MATT TRAIN

Other books by Michael Senuta:

Incident at Copper Creek
The Vengeance Brand

MATT TRAIN

•

Michael Senuta

AVALON BOOKS
NEW YORK

Published by Thomas Bouregy & Co., Inc.
160 Madison Avenue, New York, NY 10016

Library of Congress Cataloging-in-Publication Data

Senuta, Michael.
    Matt Train / Michael Senuta.
        p. cm.
    ISBN 978-0-8034-9921-8 (acid-free paper)
    I. Title.

    PS3569.E63M38   2008
    813'.54—dc22

                                2008023514

PRINTED IN THE UNITED STATES OF AMERICA
ON ACID-FREE PAPER
BY HADDON CRAFTSMEN, BLOOMSBURG, PENNSYLVANIA

Chapter One

Della Dorn stirred uneasily as she attempted to move into a sitting position. Her shoulder pained her deeply, and her left arm felt numb. For a long minute she did not know where she was.

A ray of sunlight found its way through the stagecoach window, but the window was in the wrong place, or rather, she was in the wrong place. She shook her head in order to clear it, focused her eyes, and realized that the stage was on its side, and she was sitting atop one of the doors.

She looked down at her hand as though she were afraid she would not find it, but it was there, where it was supposed to be, at the end of her arm. The fact that she could not feel it concerned her, but at least it was still there, still a part of her. Little by little, she checked the rest of her body and found that everything appeared to be intact, although as she sat, her head began to spin and her ears started to ring.

She looked about the empty coach. It seemed foreign to her, as though she had never seen it before, but when she spotted her handbag and her parasol, she felt some degree of reassurance, and she began to remember.

She ran her hand across her face and felt a large bump on her forehead, just below her hairline. The skin was sensitive, and she moaned loudly, although she doubted that anyone cared, for no one appeared to be around. She recalled that there had been another passenger—a man dressed in a business suit. Where had he gone? Perhaps, she concluded, he had been thrown clear.

Five minutes later, after some of the spin had left her head, she decided she had to climb out of the stage. She was almost afraid to see what lay outside, but she knew she could not remain where she was. She could do herself no good here. Besides, there might be others who were hurt, in need of assistance.

Gingerly, she stood up. Her legs proved to be uninjured. Her next problem would be to raise herself in order to climb through the window. There was a hand strap just to the side of the door. She reached up with her right hand and gripped it. She attempted to pull herself up using one hand but it was no use. Her left hand, still without feeling, was needed if she were to succeed. She began to massage her hand, flexing her muscles and moving her fingers. Soon, she felt the sensation of pins and needles, and slowly her control began to return. Although her grip was still tenuous, she believed that if she relied on the strength of her right arm and used her left solely for leverage, she could make it through the window of the coach. She reached for her handbag and parasol. She noticed her mirror lying a few inches from her handbag. She dropped it back inside the bag and pulled the drawstring securely. She tossed her handbag through the window first, but before following it with her parasol, an idea occurred to her. If she could use the crook of her parasol as a support, it might be easier to pull herself up. She extended the parasol around the window frame. Then, she gripped the opposite end with her left hand. It was not of a sturdy construction, she realized, but it might serve to pull her up such a short distance. Gripping the strap firmly in her right hand and the parasol in her left, she bent her knees, curled her legs upward, and pointed her feet in the air. It was not the most ladylike position to be in, for her dress and petticoat had fallen back over her head. Nevertheless, she soon had her legs through the window and, relying as much as possible on her right hand and the strap, she found herself sitting on the stage door.

Pulling her parasol out after her, she caught her breath, and then, gripping the nearest wheel, managed to slide down the side of the stage. She miscalculated the distance to the ground, however, twisting her foot as she landed unceremoniously in a heap. She grunted in disgust at her clumsiness but also managed a smile at her triumph in extricating herself from the stage. Climbing to her feet, she straightened out her undergarments and her dress. With her first step, she felt a sharp pain in her left ankle. Leaning against the stage, she raised her foot and turned her ankle in short circles. It was not bad, she concluded, but walking could be difficult for the next few days.

She quickly surveyed the area around the overturned coach. The horses were nowhere in sight. The driver was lying on the ground some fifty feet away. The other passenger, an elderly man in a dark suit, lay not far from the driver. Della scanned the landscape but saw nothing but sand, scrub, and a few clusters of ocotillo. Save for a slight breeze, there was nothing moving in the immediate vicinity or in the distance. Judging from the sun's position in the sky, she gauged that she had been unconscious for at least two hours.

Slowly, Della made her way to the driver. He lay on his side, his arms and legs at awkward angles. The front of his shirt was covered in blood. Della knelt down and felt his skin. He was cold to the touch. Next, she moved to the body of the passenger. He, too, looked awkward on the ground, his face resting on the sand, his back twisted in an exaggerated position. Gently, she turned him over. A pained expression was etched on his face. A pair of holes had pierced his shirt and suit. His clothes were also covered in blood. She had seen death before, but it was never easy to look at, regardless of the circumstances.

Della stood up and turned away—half in anger, half in fear. She was alone now—on the road, far from any town.

There was no one to carry her luggage or to assist her in any way. There was no one with whom to talk, no one with whom to commiserate. She was, she realized, utterly alone. For a moment, panic seized her. After she regained control, she organized her thoughts. She could not remain where she was. The stage may not be missed for some time. Furthermore, the chance of anyone happening by so far from any civilization was remote.

She decided to walk on in the same direction the stage had been traveling. There would surely be a way station ahead—perhaps not more than ten miles or so—and her destination, the town of Questor, could not be that far beyond. With a tender ankle, it would be difficult, but she concluded that she had little choice.

She would need water. Surely, the driver would have carried some. She made her way back to the stage, where she immediately located a canteen just beneath the driver's seat. She picked it up and a swishing sound told her that it was about half full. She wished for a drink now, but her instinct told her that she should conserve it. She adjusted the canteen strap around her shoulder. She then searched for a rifle. There was none. She had noticed earlier that the passenger had not been wearing a gun and holster. She believed that the driver was.

As she turned to walk in his direction, she froze in her tracks. Standing before her, not more than ten feet away, was a young Apache warrior. He wore a red headband, a drab-looking loose shirt, buckskin breeches, and moccasins. His face was swarthy, his nose was flat, and his hair and eyes were the color of a raven's wing. He stared at Della, wearing a mingled expression of curiosity and menace.

Della's mouth opened in stunned surprise, sudden fear gripping her. She did not know whether to run or fight, yet how could she fight? She glanced beyond the Apache at the body of the driver, now so far away. With the warrior standing between her and the driver, she had no chance to obtain the weapon. Perhaps, Della thought, the Apache intended her no harm. Perhaps he was merely inquisitive. Such a theory was shattered when he drew a knife from the sheath in his sash and advanced toward her.

Della gasped as she stepped away from him. She knew that outrunning him was an impossibility. Even if her ankle were sound, she was not dressed for speed. She continued to move away until her back nudged against the stage. He continued to advance until he was only five feet away. An idea occurred to her. She slipped the canteen from her shoulder, took firm hold of the strap, and swung it at the Apache. Startled by the sudden defense she employed, he leaped away, gave her a searching look, and then grinned in the way a cat would eye a mouse. He advanced again, more cautiously this time, as he shifted his knife from hand to hand. Della wielded the canteen again, recklessly, with little design for accuracy. In fact, she swung so hard, the weight of the canteen nearly caused her to stumble.

The scene played out for a full minute, with the

Apache seeming to enjoy himself while Della was at her wits' end as she struggled to keep him at bay. Finally, the warrior grew weary of the game as the expression on his face turned serious. He bobbed and weaved and then suddenly lunged forward, the knife extended in his hand. Della moved backward until she could retreat no more.

It was then that a shot rang out. The knife flew from the Apache's hand and he gripped his wrist, pain masking his face. For a long moment, he just stood there, statuelike, as though he failed to comprehend the situation. Then he looked over his shoulder. Della turned as well and saw a rider in the distance, approaching at a fast gait. The young warrior spun on his feet and ran. He almost flew across the sand, disappearing over a rise. An instant later, Della saw him riding away on a pony.

Della breathed a sigh of relief as she dropped the canteen on the ground and turned to face the new arrival. It was a man on a big roan, moving toward her steadily but with a caution borne of living in the land of the Apache. When he neared the stage, he dismounted with a smooth rhythm in his form and a bearing that defied his size. He was a big man, at least two hundred twenty pounds that were evenly distributed over a six-foot-two frame. His Stetson was sweat-stained and a bit battered, its leather strings dangling loosely on either side of his face, meeting at a point below his chin. In his left hand he held a Winchester; on his hip was a .45, cradled in a holster that was tied down low on his thigh. His eyes flitted back and forth until they reached the body of the other passenger.

Immediately, he made his way to the lifeless form and began to search through his pockets. Finding nothing, he muttered something to himself and then moved directly to the stage, passing within a few feet of Della without speaking a word to her. He climbed atop one of the wheels and peered into the coach. He then jumped down and quickly maneuvered around the other side of the stage. In a moment, he reappeared and faced Della.

"Was the other passenger carrying a valise . . . some luggage . . . anything?" he asked, a tone of desperation in his voice.

Totally taken aback by such a question, Della stammered, "I . . . uh . . . no, I don't think so."

"Are you certain?" he asked, his eyes boring into hers.

"Yes, I'm certain. When he boarded the stage, he wasn't carrying anything."

His jaw tightened. "What happened here?"

"I . . . I don't know exactly. There were some shots. I heard the driver yell at the horses. The stage lurched and then it overturned. I must have been knocked unconscious. When I came to, I managed to climb out of the coach. I found things exactly the way they are now."

The man nodded. He whistled to his horse. The roan loped forward, coming to a halt a few feet away from him. The man placed the Winchester in its scabbard and loosened his blanket roll. He unfurled it and draped it gently over the body of the passenger. Then he returned to his horse and swung into the saddle. "Mount up behind me, miss. We have to be on the move."

"But . . . who are you?"

"There's no time for formal introductions. We're likely to have company any time now."

Della looked around but saw no signs of life. "If you mean that young Indian, I doubt that he's going to come back."

"I'm gambling that he will . . . with reinforcements. Three of his friends are camped not more than two miles from here."

Della was uncertain. "Will you take me to town?"

"Not directly, but I'll see that you get to safety by and by."

"What about my portmanteau?"

"Not where we're going. We have to travel light and fast."

Della was in a quandary. She did not know anything about this man, yet he had saved her life. She decided that she had to trust him. She retrieved her handbag, wound the drawstring securely around her wrist, and made her way to the roan. On its flank, she noticed a brand—two horizontal lines crossed by three evenly spaced vertical ones. There was something vaguely familiar about it, yet she could not place it. She did not have long to consider it, however, for the man suddenly reached down, took her by the arm, and swung her up behind him. He spurred the roan, and the big horse bolted off. Della barely had time to wrap her arms around the man's chest. In what seemed like a matter of seconds, they were far from the wrecked stage and heading north. Della glanced over her shoulder and saw no sign of activity behind them. She did not know whether the Apaches would be following them or not. She did not know where they were headed, only that the next way station lay to the west. She bit her lower lip as she held firmly to the strange man and wondered exactly what she was getting herself into.

They rode for more than an hour without conversing. Della was uncomfortable and ill-prepared to be on the back of a horse. Her dress made the journey awkward, but she held onto the stranger snugly and endured the ride as best she could. The terrain was mostly flat, with some occasional hillocks and clusters of huge rocks. Cactus, a smattering of wild flowers, and whip-like strands of ocotillo dotted the land. After a time, Della noticed a slight incline in the terrain as the horse labored a bit more and her vision of the landscape took on a different perspective. They were at a considerably higher elevation now. She could see for miles in every direction save straight ahead, where the ridge of a tall spine of rock twisted in front of them at a long, sweeping angle, disappearing somewhere off in the distance at a point she could not determine.

The stranger picked his way through ravines and around rocks with a certitude that amazed her. He appeared to know every inch of ground by heart. At one point they crossed a small stream, where they paused for the first time. Here, he allowed the horse to drink as he scanned the landscape in every direction. He did not leave the saddle and still he did not speak, for he seemed intent on reaching a destination known only to him. Finally, after the horse had swallowed his share from the streambed, the man urged him on, continuing in the same direction until the light was chased from the sky and long shadows began to stretch across the land.

A short time later, the man pulled into a dry wash, where he reined in the roan and glanced from left to right. Apparently satisfied with whatever it was that concerned him, he turned and said, "We'll camp here for the night."

Della was a bit startled. "Camp . . . here?"

He extended his arm. Reluctantly, she took it, and he helped her swing down.

She stretched her arms and legs and massaged the small of her back, for her muscles had been tense ever since the attack on the stage and her ordeal with the young Apache. Furthermore, the long horseback ride had aggravated her aches and pains.

The man swung down from the roan and led it to a nearby thicket, where he secured the reins.

Della looked about anxiously. "What about the Apaches? Won't they find us here?"

"The Apaches don't come this far. They're superstitious about this ground."

"Oh, I see." But she really did not.

"I'll gather some wood and start a fire. Can you make coffee?" he asked.

"Of course I can make coffee."

He frowned. "In the saddlebags . . . you'll find what you need. There's water in the canteen. There's some jerky as well." He started down the wash.

Della felt uneasy as she shot a series of glances at the gathering shadows, but she stepped to the roan and began rummaging through the saddlebags. The big horse turned his head, gave her an inquisitive look, then turned away and started to nibble at a clump of brown grass.

Five minutes later, the man returned with an armful of sticks of various sizes. He built a fire, and Della prepared the coffee.

The coffee, Della admitted to herself, was very good. It was hot and soothing, and it helped to relieve her fatigue. The jerky, though tough and stringy, was nutritious and made her realize just how hungry she was.

They ate in silence for several minutes before the man finally spoke. "Train," he said.

Della eyed him curiously and then stared into the distance, listening for a sound.

"My name," he added, smiling at her.

"Your . . . name?"

"Matt Train. We didn't have time for any formalities back at the stage."

"Oh. It's nice to meet you, Mr. Train." She felt a little silly. She considered his name and then remembered the brand on the roan, realizing that it symbolized a railroad track. She regarded him closer. "I believe I recall the name . . . from an earlier visit to Questor. In fact, I think

I even saw you once—it would have been about two years ago. You looked considerably different then. You were dressed in a suit, and you seemed—well, forgive me for saying so—much younger."

Train took a sip from his cup. "Time and events have a way of aging a man."

Uncertain as to what he meant, Della continued. "There was a celebration at the hotel restaurant—for your parents as I recollect."

Train nodded, a wistful look in his eyes. "That would have been my parents' anniversary . . . but I don't recall ever seeing you before."

"It's not likely that you would have. I live in St. Louis with my father or, at least, I did. My father passed away about six months ago. I come to the town of Questor on occasion to visit my aunt. Maybe you know her. She runs the millinery."

"Marion Vale?"

"That's right."

He nodded. "I know her. She's a good woman."

Della smiled. "I'm Della Dorn."

"It's nice to meet you, Della, regardless of the circumstances."

"I believe my aunt mentioned that your family owns the biggest ranch in the territory."

Train's jaw tightened as though someone had stuck a knife in him and twisted it. He nodded and then reached for the coffeepot.

Della felt she had said something wrong and decided

to change the subject. "Matt, my aunt will be worried about me when the stage fails to arrive. Will you be able to take me to town tomorrow?"

"No."

"But . . . I don't understand."

"I'll see that you get to the way station. From there, you can catch the next stage to Questor."

"Why can't you take me yourself?"

"It isn't safe just now—for either of us."

"You mean the Apaches?"

"Them . . . and the whites as well."

"I don't know what you mean."

He took a swallow from his cup. "I might as well tell you now. You'll find out sooner or later. I can't return to town. I'm wanted."

She was so taken aback that she nearly dropped her cup. "Wanted? Do you mean to say you're an outlaw?"

"There are some who would consider me as such. The legal powers that be certainly do."

"Well, I don't believe it. Your family is the wealthiest in the territory. From what I understood from my aunt, you're certainly among the most respected people around."

"I still believe that there are those who respect us, but a new breed has come to Questor, a new force that has worked against my family and against the law as we know it."

Della stared at Train in disbelief. "Why are you wanted?"

"For murder."

"Murder!" she uttered, stunned. "I can't believe that you could murder anybody."

"I didn't, but that's not the point. The evidence and the witnesses tell a different story."

She placed her cup on a rock. "What happened?"

He pushed back his Stetson and cradled his cup in his hands. "It's a long story, one that I don't rightly believe myself."

"Who was killed?"

"Ed Marbury, the sheriff of Questor, and his deputy, Rad Barlow."

"Go on."

"I had nothing to do with Marbury's death, but I did kill Rad Barlow."

She looked at him askance.

"But it wasn't murder. He was trying to kill my father."

"Kill your father? Why on earth would a lawman want to do that?"

"Because he was corrupt and greedy, and he was acting on orders from a man named Clegg Ralston."

"Who's Clegg Ralston?"

"He's a big man in Questor who wants to be bigger. In fact, he wants everything—including the Train Ranch. Not only has he framed me for murder, he's framed my father as well. My family has been on the run for over a month now."

Della shook her head. "This must all be like a nightmare for you."

"That it is, a nightmare that I keep telling myself I'll break free of, but the darkness doesn't end."

"Isn't there anything you can do to prove your innocence? Can't you hire a lawyer?"

Train placed his cup on the ground. "Ben Connover, our family lawyer and friend, worked hard to clear us, but it was difficult. We could never meet openly. We communicated through a few loyal friends . . . at night . . . in secluded places. He was watched constantly, both by the law and by Ralston's men. Two weeks ago, Ben left town to follow a lead. He sent word through a friend that he had uncovered information that would discredit Ralston and enable my family to take the necessary steps to clear our name. He was returning to Questor with that information."

"What was the information?" Della asked.

Train frowned. "I don't know. He never made it back."

She regarded him quizzically.

"He was on the stage with you."

Della assessed his remark. "The other passenger— the elderly man in the suit?" she gasped.

"That's right. Whoever waylaid the stage removed whatever documents he carried. I searched through his pockets and found nothing and, as you indicated, he had no luggage."

"But why would Apaches do such a thing?"

"The Apaches didn't waylay the stage. It was Ralston's men. Whatever information Ben Connover carried they now have."

Della sat in silence for a long moment as she digested Train's story. "I understand now why you placed your blanket over him. He was your friend. I watched you carefully, and yet you did nothing for the driver."

"Perhaps I should have. After all, he was dead. It would have been the Christian thing to do. At the time, however, I felt no sympathy for him."

"But why not?"

"Because the driver was in on the ambush. He brought about his own death as well as the death of Ben Connover."

"But how do you know that?"

"I was going to meet the stage at a point not far from where it was attacked. Ben was going to ride with me to meet up with my parents to discuss the evidence he had turned up and to develop a strategy to use in court. I had a horse for him but it came up lame with a stone bruise, and I was delayed. I would have been able to avert the attack on the stage if the driver would have kept to his regular route. Instead, he took an old side road that led him to what could only have been a prearranged spot— where Ralston's men were waiting in ambush."

"But the driver was killed as well."

"Either there was a falling out, or he was double-crossed. Any way you look at it, they left no witnesses. Most likely, they thought you were dead."

"That's incredible."

"These men are ruthless. They'll stop at nothing to get what they want, and there's a fortune at stake."

"I don't know what to say."

"There's nothing you can say. There's nothing you can do. Just try to get some sleep. In the morning you'll ride with me to meet up with my parents. It's only a few hours away, but moving over these rocks in the dark is too risky, even for Bullwhip. Besides, I'm not in any hurry to get there. I don't relish giving the news about Ben Connover to my folks. They've been expecting good news—the first we've had since all this started, but it has to be done."

She nodded.

Train made his way to the roan and removed a leather coat from his saddlebag. He stepped over to Della and draped it over her shoulders. "This should keep you warm enough tonight."

"Thanks. What about you?"

"I'll sit near the fire."

She stretched out on the ground and pulled the coat more snugly around her. She watched him for a long time as he sat there a few yards away, occasionally feeding twigs to the small flames. Though his face was troubled, there was a strong resolve etched into it. A soft-spoken, brooding man, he seemed to be possessed of a deep inner strength that spurred him on. She turned over in her mind everything he had related to her and, fantastic as it all was, she concluded that she believed every word of it. He had saved her life. For that alone, she was grateful. She determined that if there were anything that she could do to help him, she would find a way. In time, her eyelids grew heavy, and she could concentrate no more. The flames from the campfire became a soft blur, and she drifted off to sleep.

Chapter Two

Della stirred uneasily. Her muscles were sore and aching after spending the night on the hard ground. Her left wrist, in particular, the one she hurt when the stage overturned, throbbed miserably. She massaged it gently as she sat up and looked around. Matt Train was still sitting in front of the fire, in almost the same position when she had last seen him. Steam was escaping from the coffeepot, and the aroma of a fresh brew filled the air. The first rays of the sun were filtering through the clouds, painting a pleasant canvas of colors across the sky. It was still cool, but the air was warming quickly, and the land would soon be baking in the full light of day. Della removed the leather coat and folded it neatly beside her. She eyed Train closely, recalling the events of the previous day and wondering if everything had actually happened as she remembered.

"Good morning," Train said, his back still partially turned toward her.

"Good morning," Della replied.

"You slept well."

"I . . . I did? I was so tired I don't believe I stirred an inch all night."

He filled a cup, strolled over, and handed it to her.

She cradled it in her hands. The metal cup was hot and warmed her fingers. The coffee was blazing hot. She blew on it for a moment and then risked a sip. It was strong and tasty, and it warmed her insides. "It's good," she said.

"Not too strong?"

"Oh, no . . . well, a little maybe."

He smiled. "As soon as you feel up to it, we'll be riding."

"Whatever you say." She continued to sip at the coffee as she watched him step around the fire. He was light on his feet for such a big man. There was an economy in his movement, a deliberateness about everything he did. She regarded him curiously as he removed the pot and kicked dirt onto the fire. "You're not having any coffee?" she asked.

"I had mine."

She glanced about but saw no other cup. Suddenly, she felt guilty, for he must have been out of supplies and had given her the last of the grounds. "Actually, it is a little strong for me. There's not much more than a swallow or two left. I hate to waste it. Would you like to finish it?"

He hesitated but finally walked over to her. He sat down beside her and took the cup, draining it in one draught. "I guess maybe it is a little strong at that. My father and I like it that way. My mother doesn't. She usually makes it to suit us."

Della smiled. She ran her hand through her hair and pushed back a strand that dangled over her forehead. "I must look a sight," she said self-consciously.

"I'd say you look mighty fine. I don't think I've ever seen a girl with red hair exactly like yours before."

"It's auburn, actually."

"It's very pretty."

Della felt herself blush as she climbed to her feet and tried to smooth out her dress.

Within minutes, they were mounted and on their way. For the next two hours, they wound their way through narrow ravines and deep canyons, around huge boulders and across deposits of shattered rocks. Della felt hopelessly lost, but their journey finally seemed to be at an end as Train steered the roan into a small clearing, where they came upon a stone hut with two horses tied a short distance off to one side. It appeared to be an old structure, for the stones were cracked in many places and heavily weathered. A thin worm of smoke emanated from a chimney near one corner of the roof.

Train helped Della dismount and then slid out of the saddle himself. He tied the roan next to the other horses and took Della's arm. Just before they reached the hut, the door opened and a man and woman emerged. The man looked to be about sixty-five. He was tall, a little sloped in the shoulders, and had gray hair and a thick gray mustache. He carried a Winchester. The woman looked to be a bit younger. Her hair was black, but tinged with streaks of gray. She was thin, and although her face was drawn, her features were fine. At one time she must have been very beautiful. The resemblance between the two of them and Train was obvious.

"Welcome back, son," the man said.

The woman smiled warmly.

"Hello, Mother, Pa," Matt said with a smile.

"Well, what's this?" the man asked as he eyed Della. "I send you to collect Ben Connover, and you come back with a pretty girl."

Matt grinned. "This is Miss Della Dorn. Miss Dorn, my mother and father."

"I'm pleased to meet you," Della said.

"Welcome, Della. I'm Mort Train, and this is my wife, Sarah," the man said with a smile.

"My dear, you must be very weary from the terrible journey that brought you here. Please come in for something to eat," Sarah said, placing her arm around Della and ushering her into the hut.

"Trouble, Matt?" Mort asked, his face heavy with worry.

"Yes, Pa. Bad trouble. Ben's dead."

Mort shook his head. He bit his lip as he turned

toward the hut. "This isn't going to be easy on your mother. You'd best come in and tell us about it."

Matt nodded as he followed his father inside.

The interior of the hut was dimly lit. There were only a few essentials—some wooden chairs, a table, a small cabinet stacked with some dishes, and a shelf of food-stuffs, mostly airtights. They all sat down at the table as Matt took the next five minutes to explain to his parents about the attack on the stage and the murder of Ben Connover. His father showed little emotion, but his mother nearly broke into tears. She lowered her head and cradled her face in her hands. Mort placed a soothing hand on her shoulder, and she perked up, regained her composure, and smiled.

"All is not lost, Mother. We may not have the evidence Ben discovered, but on the other hand, we know that that evidence does exist—and if Ben found it, so can we."

"But how will we go about it, Matt?" she asked.

"I don't know yet, but there are other lawyers in other towns. We have to make contact with one that we can trust and somehow follow Ben's lead."

"That makes sense, son," Mort said. "There's Joe Winston over in Grandville. I've done business with him before. He's a good man. If we can get him on our side, we have a chance."

"It's worth a try. I can ride over there as soon as I get Della back to her aunt in Questor."

Sarah glanced at Della. "Dorn . . . you don't mean to say that Marion Vale is your aunt?"

"That's right."

Sarah beamed. "Why, she's a good friend of mine. You'll have to give her my best."

"I'll be sure to do that, Mrs. Train."

"On second thought, Mother, it might not be wise for Della to tell anyone else of her encounter with us. Any connection to us could arouse a number of awkward questions."

"Of course. There are times when I forget that we're wanted by the law. Any association with the Train family could place you in danger."

"I understand."

"Well, I don't imagine that the two of you have had any breakfast. I'll fix something right away," Sarah announced.

"Thank you, Mrs. Train. I am rather hungry."

In no time at all, Sarah had coffee, bacon, and beans on the table. She fussed over everything and did her best to make Della feel at home. While Della and Matt ate, she and Mort sat opposite them. "You'll have to forgive these rude surroundings and the poor table I've set before you. The truth of the matter is that our supplies are limited. If you had chanced to visit us at a time not so long ago, you would have enjoyed a first-rate meal served on linen," Sarah explained.

"It's a fine meal, Mrs. Train, and the company makes up for the lack of luxury."

"Those are kind remarks," Mort said with a smile.

"Indeed they are," Sarah added. "You're a good girl,"

she said, patting Della's hand. "You've had a bad experience."

"It doesn't seem like much more than the blink of an eye compared to what you people are going through."

"It's been bad, all right. I can't call it anything else," Mort said. "We've been in hiding, on the run, living like hunted animals for quite a spell now. Sarah, here, has braved up well, considering. I wanted to send her back East to be with her sister, out of harm's way, but she wouldn't have it."

"My place is with you, Mortimer," Sarah replied, casting a loving look at him.

"Matt told me generally about what happened, but he didn't give me the whole story," Della stated.

Mort folded his hands on the table before him and took a deep breath. "Well, it's a long story, but an old one, as old as mankind. It's about greed mostly and what some folks will do to get what they want."

Taking a sip of her coffee, Della said, "Matt mentioned a Clegg Ralston."

Mort nodded. "He's the one behind this matter, him and his men—a passel of no-accounts that would give a pack of wolves a good name in comparison."

"He's the reason you can't return to your spread?"

"He is. Until this mess is cleared up, it isn't safe for us to set foot on our own land."

"If that ever happens," Sarah intoned with a sigh.

"It will, Mother, it will," Matt said reassuringly.

Mort smiled. "Della, I came to this territory over forty

years ago with not much more than the clothes on my back. I tried my hand at a little bit of everything—freighting, prospecting. I built this hut way back then when I was digging holes in the sides of mountains, searching for gold that wasn't to be found. I didn't know that it would come in handy this many years later. I didn't imagine it would still be standing, but it is. I finally set my mind to ranching. I staked out my claim—the richest valley within a hundred miles—prime land, good for beef. I met Sarah, we fell in love, and we married. We built our home, settled down, and prospered. Matt came along—our only son, but a fine one.

"It was a hard life but a good one. The people here got along, worked side by side, that is, until about a year ago when Clegg Ralston showed up. He calls himself a businessman—works as a cattle broker, sells a little real estate. He's as slick as they come. He's got a bunch of gunmen on his payroll who like to intimidate people. One of my hands caught a few of his men trying to rustle some of our horses. I pressed charges, but Judge Foster dismissed them. He claimed there was insufficient evidence—the word of one of my men against the word of two of Ralston's men. Judge Foster and I had it out in court, a regular shouting match it was. He fined me for contempt. That's the day that Ralston must have gotten the idea to start his plan in motion. Two days after the hearing, Judge Foster was murdered. His body was found on my spread. Everybody knew that there were hard feelings between us. I never did like the old buzzard. I admit it. I always thought he was too soft, and I never regretted that I let him know about it, but I never would have laid a hand on him. I have too much respect for the law to do such a thing. Well, since everybody remembered the hard words we had for each other in court, I was the natural suspect of many people. Oh, the old-timers knew that I would never have a hand in such a thing, but the newer people in the territory weren't so sure. I can't say that I blame them, considering what happened.

"It was Ed Marbury, our local sheriff and a good man, who came out to the ranch house with news of the judge's killing. He wanted me to accompany him to town for the inquest. Well, I didn't think anything of it. I had known Marbury for years. He told me himself that he never even remotely believed that I had anything to do with Judge Foster's death, but there was some talk—no doubt fanned by Clegg Ralston—and for appearance's sake, he asked me to ride into town to assist in the investigation. I tend to blow up once in a while, as I did in court, but when the dust settles I'm a reasonable man. It was a straightforward request, and I honored it.

"We weren't more than a mile off my spread, however, when we were surrounded by Rad Barlow, who was Marbury's deputy; Steve Payton and Webb Crane, some local businessmen; and three of Ralston's gunmen. At first, they claimed they were there to help guard me, but the sheriff would have none of it. An argument broke out, and one of Ralston's men—Burl Archer—shot and killed Sheriff Marbury. It all happened so suddenly I was stunned, as were Payton and Crane, but I quickly realized that Barlow and Ralston's men had planned the whole thing all along. It didn't take long for Ralston's men to come up with the idea of stringing me up on the spot. Well, Payton and Crane were white with shock. They knew that the entire matter had gotten out of hand. Even so, they were powerless to do anything about it. They were no hands with guns. Besides, they weren't even armed. I was carrying no sidearm, and Barlow pulled my Winchester from its scabbard before I could react. In no time at all I found myself under a tree. My hands were tied behind me, and there was a noose around my neck. Barlow raised his hand and was a second away from swatting my horse out from under me when a shot rang out. Barlow toppled from his saddle and struck the ground. He stirred for a moment and then never moved again. The others looked around, panicked, and then rode off. Fortunately, Matt had followed after me. His sure shot with a Winchester had saved me from being strung up."

"Just as he saved me from that Apache brave yesterday," Della added, casting an admiring look at Matt.

Matt shifted uneasily in his chair.

"But what happened wasn't through any fault of yours, Mr. Train," Della said.

"That's true enough, but the way I told you everything happened isn't the way the story came out. Matt and I were going to go into town later that day with the bodies of Ed Marbury and Rad Barlow to get things cleared up, but a bad storm was brewing. We decided to make the trip in the morning but we never got the chance. A mob came to our ranch house that evening. It must have been twenty strong. Better than half of them were Ralston's men, and Ralston himself was leading the pack. They demanded that Matt and I turn ourselves over to them. Such a move would have been suicide. After what they tried to do to me earlier in the day, I had no intention of putting Matt and myself in their hands. We talked back and forth, with Ralston doing most of the palavering. Well, it turned out that the real facts as to what happened earlier got a little twisted. Ralston claimed that Matt and I had killed the sheriff and deputy in cold blood when they came out to arrest me for the murder of Judge Foster."

"But surely the townsmen who knew you didn't believe such a thing? After all, your reputation is well founded," Della said.

Mort shrugged. "Most didn't. A few straddled the fence—and Ralston did his best to push them onto his side. The cold, hard facts were that Judge Foster, Sheriff Marbury, and Deputy Barlow were all dead, and when you've got three dead men, there's got to be retribution. I was connected to all three deaths, and Matt was connected to two. I tried to explain exactly what happened, but Ralston's men told a different story, and Payton and Crane backed them up. They were leaky vessels, both of them. Besides, intimidation and liquor go a long way toward pushing some people into doing things they wouldn't normally do."

"What happened then?"

"Well, I've never been one to violate the law, but since there was no longer any formal authority left in Questor, I told them to summon the US marshal in Warrensburg, and that we'd surrender ourselves to him. That wasn't good enough for them, and they opened up on us. Ordinarily, we would have had the hands to force them off the spread, but with most of our boys away on a cattle drive we had only a few on the premises. They were easily overpowered by the mob and badly beaten. Matt and I were able to stand the lot of them off for quite a spell—until they set fire to the house. That was when we had no choice but to run. Sarah was home, and her safety was our responsibility. As I said, there was a bad storm brewing. The sky was heavy with clouds, and the moon was completely hidden. We were able to slip out a back window. Matt managed to secure three horses from one of our corrals, and we had little difficulty in escaping through the hills that border our ranch house in the rear. High winds, rain, and streaks of lightning made the going dicey at times. The horses were skittish. Sometimes there are flash floods in those foothills, but nobody knows the terrain there better than Matt and I do, and we put considerable distance between us and the mob."

"There was no way they could follow us at night in that storm," Matt added. "By morning, we were ten miles away and in one of our line shacks. After that, we kept on the move, retreating farther and farther into the mountains until we ended up here."

Mort shook his head in despair. "I've never turned tail and run away from any man, and I was never forced from my own spread before."

"There, there, Mort, you were only thinking of me," Sarah said as she patted his hand.

Mort nodded and forced a smile, but Sarah's attempt to rationalize the situation seemed small consolation to him.

"Then your ranch house was burned to the ground?" Della asked.

"No, we have the heavy rains from the storm to thank for that, but there was considerable damage to the roof and one wall. It's going to take some major repair," Matt explained. "I return at night from time to time to remove clothes and other essentials we need to survive. There are guards posted, but I usually have no problem in slipping past them."

Mort grinned. "Matt can crawl under an Apache's legs if he has a mind to. No townsfolk would ever see him if he doesn't want to be seen."

"The last time I was there I didn't see anyone. I guess they figure we wouldn't have the nerve to risk returning with half the town on the lookout for us."

"They also ran off our stock," Sarah put in. "We can't go home, and there are wanted posters on both Mort and Matt."

"But we've got a few cards to play," Mort said. "We were able to send a wire, through Ben Connover, to the hotel where our hands will be staying once they reach the rail head. They should be arriving any time now. They've got orders to hole up at Lawton Wells, a town about half a day's ride from here, until I send for them. I don't want them riding into a trap when they return. If this confrontation turns into an all-out war, they'll back us up when we need them."

"And we have many loyal friends in town," Sarah added. "If it comes down to it, I'm certain they will stand by us."

"Yeah, but there are plenty of guns out there who are doing their level best to make sure that we won't even see the inside of a jail cell let alone a courtroom, and Clegg Ralston's chief among them," Mort explained.

"Well, with the sheriff and his deputy gone, who is the law in Questor now?" Della asked.

"A man by the name of Dub Parker, one of Ralston's cronies," Matt replied. "Ralston managed to influence the town council to appoint Parker temporarily until the next election. Parker, in turn, has deputized some of Ralston's men to ride with him."

"I'm sorry to find you in this situation, and I'm sorry that we had to meet under these circumstances." Della sighed. "I wish there was something I could do to help."

Matt splayed his fingers on the table. "Our best chance is to get Webb Crane to change his story, but we can't locate him. For that matter, he's probably lying dead in a ditch somewhere, suffering the same fate as Steve Payton."

"Payton is dead?" Della asked, surprised.

Matt nodded. "They found him at the bottom of an arroyo. His neck was broken. They said it was an accident, that his horse must have stumbled. He drank a lot."

"But it's quite a coincidence that one of the witnesses against you was killed, and the other has disappeared."

"Yes, it is, isn't it?" Sarah said with a knowing smile.

"What about the other men who set out to hang you? Couldn't they be forced to tell the truth?"

"Only at the point of a gun, and that wouldn't go far to convince anybody," Mort explained. "It certainly wouldn't do in a court of law—if things got that far. Once under the protection of the court, they would only lie again."

"We also have to get a legitimate lawman to take charge," Matt put in. "Only then will we have a chance of beating Ralston at his own game."

"Ben Connover wired to Marshal Frank Weldon in Warrensburg, explaining the situation, but at this point we don't know if he's arrived in Questor yet."

"But what does Ralston hope to gain by all this?" Della asked.

Mort frowned. "He wants the Train Ranch. That's why he's framed Matt and me for murder. He's burned us out and he's got us on the run. We can't even defend our own land while we're hiding in these mountains."

"To add to that, property taxes are due in about a week. Without making payment, we'll be in default, and our land will go up for sheriff's sale," Sarah explained.

"And that's exactly what Ralston is waiting for," Matt said.

"Is the money a problem?"

"Oh, we've got the money, but wanted men can't go near the bank. We can't even put to use the sale from our cattle. The herd alone should bring in ten times the tax assessment. The problem is how do we pay it? We'd be shot on sight if we got near the county tax assessor. Ralston's lying in wait."

"Can't you have someone else make the payment on your behalf?"

"Ordinarily, yes. Ben Connover would have handled it but with him gone, well, we just don't have the right to ask anyone else—even if there was someone who would step forward. It's too dangerous. No, Della, this is our fight, pure and simple. We can't risk losing any more of our friends, at least not until we can change the odds in our favor."

Della considered the situation for a long moment. "Why don't I pay the taxes for you?"

Mort and Sarah glanced at each other and smiled.

"You're a mighty brave girl," Sarah said as she patted Della's hand, "but we could never ask you to do that."

"But why not? Clegg Ralston and his men don't know me."

"Clegg Ralston has connections everywhere. Guns and money will do that for you," Matt said. "Even if, by some remote chance, you were able to make the payment, you wouldn't get a hundred feet from the assessor's office before Ralston found out about it. There's no telling what he would do to you to find us, and we wouldn't be able to be near enough to protect you."

Della frowned as she realized just how unrealistic her suggestion had been.

"But we thank you for the offer, Della," Mort said with a smile.

Della nodded.

Mort regarded her closely. "There may just be another way you can help us though."

Della turned her attention to him.

"You can be our eyes and ears in Questor. With Ben Connover gone, information about some of the activities in town could prove useful—providing we could make contact with you."

"Why, I'd be glad to help in any way I can."

"That's not a bad idea, Mortimer," Sarah put in. "No one would suspect a visitor from out of town of having anything to do with the Trains—if, of course, we could arrange occasional meetings with Della without endangering her."

"I'm sure that could be possible," Mort said.

"Most likely, we could work something out," Matt agreed.

"What exactly should I do?"

"Listen to the general banter in the streets. Read the newspaper," Mort explained. "Without being too obvious, pick up any gossip you can about Clegg Ralston and his men. There's no telling what may be of use to us. The smallest bit of information may give us an edge."

"I'll do it."

"But you must be extremely careful of everything you do," Sarah pointed out. "Do nothing to draw attention to yourself. If you do, your life may be in danger."

"I understand."

"We'll need a place where we can make contact," Matt said as he considered the situation.

"What about your ranch house?" Della suggested. "No one knows the grounds better than you."

"No, that's too risky. It's under guard. If Ralston's men see anyone in the area, they may shoot first and ask questions later."

"What about Slim Holly's spread?" Sarah ventured. "It's isolated enough, and it's not that far from town."

"That's a solid idea, Sarah!" Mort replied.

Matt nodded. "It could work. I've been slipping in and out of Slim's place on a regular basis since we've been on the run. He's been helping us, with foodstuffs and the like. I can get there easily enough without being seen, and at the same time I can see anyone coming for quite a distance. Della could pass any information she learns on to Slim, and Slim can get it to me."

"Then, it's settled," Mort said.

Matt rubbed his hand across his chin. "It's best that I take Della to Slim's. The two of them will need to meet. That way, Slim will know that he can trust Della."

"Makes sense. When will you be leaving, son?"

"Well, I was planning on staying until noon, but it's a longer ride to Slim's spread. We should leave soon."

"Della should get some rest first," Sarah interjected.

"I'm all right, Mrs. Train."

"Are you up to a long ride?" Sarah asked.

"I can do it."

"Pa, we can make better time if we take one of your mounts."

"Go ahead, son."

"Jasper came up lame—probably a stone bruise. He should be all right in a day or so. I had to leave him behind."

Mort scratched the back of his head. "By golly, in all the excitement of hearing the news about Ben and meeting Della, I plum failed to notice that Jasper was missing."

"I hate to leave you with only one horse."

"It won't be for that long."

Matt nodded.

"You'll need some supplies," Sarah said as she got up from the table.

"I'm fine, maybe just some coffee."

"You're strong and long in the saddle, Matt, but you can't expect a young lady to travel like you. You'll need some supplies. We've enough for a while," Sarah said.

Matt smiled. "I guess you're right enough."

"Your folks are fine people," Della stated as she rode beside Train.

He nodded. "Thank you."

"This must be the worst experience of their lives."

"It is. It's cut them deep. I'm not sure things will ever be the same."

"Your mother seems to be holding up well enough. At least, her spirit is strong. It's obvious that she takes great pride in you."

"I only pray that I can deliver them from this hell that we're in."

She reached out and placed her hand on his arm.

He reined in his horse, and she stopped beside him.

"I have every confidence that you can and will. You're a strong man, and you care about people—as do your parents."

He regarded her closely for a long moment. She was unlike other women he had known. She had courage and determination. She knew little about him and his family, and yet she was willing to stand beside them. She was tired, he knew, but she was willing to push on out of concern for them as well. She had qualities he did not quite comprehend, and he could not help but respect her for them. He found himself drawn to her, but he was not in a position to be able to do anything about it. Technically an outlaw, he knew it was not even safe for Della to be seen with him.

"We'd best move on. I want to reach Slim's place before dark. I've got a long ride back, and I want to make it into the mountains by nightfall."

"You'll camp alone in the mountains tonight?"

"Yes."

"Can't you stay at your friend Slim's?"

"No. That would place Slim in danger. He does enough for us as it is. We can't ask any more of him." He urged his horse forward.

"Where will you go next?" Della asked, falling in beside him.

"I have to pick up my horse that came up lame. I left him in a box canyon about an hour from where your stage was attacked. I want to get him back to my folks as soon as possible. If they have to move in a hurry, an extra horse will come in handy."

"I see."

"Then, I'll try to make contact with Joe Winston in Grandville. He may be able to take up where Ben Connover left off."

"You would think that there would be plenty of people on your side."

"There are, but they're also afraid . . . uncertain. I can't say I blame them. In a way, this isn't their fight."

"I seem to remember reading something once that a famous man wrote. He said that it's every man's duty to see justice done."

Train glanced at her. "You're an idealist, Della. Those are fine words to live by, but when it comes down to fists and guns, most men are content to stand by and let others do their fighting for them."

"You don't strike me as that kind of man . . . nor does your father."

"We're not, but then this is our fight, and we're not going to go down easily."

Della analyzed his words for some time. She knew that he was the kind of man who meant what he said.

Some time later, they reached a craggy spot overlooking a winding valley that spread before them for a mile. Train halted the horses and peered below at the lay of the land. Della could see a dust devil some half a mile away. Train fished some binoculars from his saddlebag and focused them on a slowly moving object.

"What is it, Apaches?" Della asked.

"No. My guess is that it's Snake Danford."

"One of Ralston's men?"

"No. He's a bounty hunter from up north. I've seen him in town before. He's been crisscrossing my trail for the last two weeks."

"He's after the reward on you?"

Train nodded. "He can smell money. He's an ambusher and a back shooter. Most men that he brings in he brings in over their saddles."

"Should we hide?"

"No. We're going in opposite directions. There's enough distance between us. As long as we keep this ridge between him and us, he won't have any line of sight with us."

"What about your parents? Is there any chance that he'll come across them?"

"Not much. They're too far back in the mountains.

Danford's persistent, but he doesn't do things the hard way. I think we can forget about him for the present."

Della nodded her understanding.

"The land is going to level off soon. We can pick up our pace. We should be at Slim's in a couple of hours. Can you make it?"

"I can make it," she said with a smile.

Train nodded and nudged his horse. He smiled to himself.

Chapter Three

Clegg Ralston drained his shot glass and set it on the table before him. He had a habit of drinking alone—never socially. It was one of his many peculiarities. Perhaps it was because the whiskey soothed his nerves and enabled him to think and plan, and he was always alone when he was thinking and planning. With most men, alcohol dulled the senses, numbed the brain. It was not so with him. It helped him to see things from a different perspective and gave him the nerve he needed to put his plans into motion. He ran his finger around the small ring of moisture left by the glass and stared at the amber color of the liquid, losing himself in the sensation it provided.

He was a big man—six-foot-two, barrel-chested, with dark hair and a thin mustache. At fifty-five, he had traveled far and wide and had seen many things. Seaports, boom towns, gold camps . . . they were all pieces of the puzzle that formed his past. He had been a double-dealer all his life. He had lived on the fringe of the law and had made a healthy living by cheating, stealing, forging, and even rustling. He possessed no true skills save one—the art of avoiding prison despite having led a life of deceit and corruption.

He had been known by several names, each of which he had blemished. Despite, however, his long list of crimes, he had resorted to murder only once. It was three years ago, in Denver, where his involvement in a fraudulent cattle deal had been discovered by another confidence man. Since it was a violation of his code to pay tribute to a fellow professional, he killed him and fled, adopting a new name and a new line, but still in-grained with his same taste for larceny.

Having left Denver in his wake, he took a hundred twisted roads until he found himself in Questor—a small community that was the home of one of the most suc-cessful ranchers in the state. Ralston always thought big, and he saw dollar signs every time Mort Train rode into town. Many an hour he dreamed and schemed his way into Train's boots, but he saw no feasible way of parlay-ing his small stake and bag of confidence tricks into ob-taining a piece of the Train Ranch until, that is, some of his men got caught up in his rustling operation. One thing led to another until Train's argument with the local judge gave Ralston the opportunity he needed to put his plan into action. In fact, his scheme had worked out better than

he expected. Eliminating Train in a lynching had back-
fired, but he had been able to lay the blame for the killings
of both the sheriff and deputy on Train and his son.

He believed that, in the end, all of the Trains, including Sarah, could be eliminated, and he had come within
a hair's breadth of accomplishing that on the night that
he and the mob he had whipped up had set fire to the
Train ranch house. He had been disappointed at their escape, but now the entire family was on the run. Both father and son were wanted by the law, primed by a pack
of lies and a select group of witnesses to be shot on
sight. It would be best if Ralston took no hand in the
matter personally. There was no reason for him to do so,
for he had time and numbers on his side—big numbers.
He had managed to convince certain elements of the
town of Questor of the Trains' guilt. The majority of
residents, he realized, would never believe the Trains
were guilty of anything, but there were some who were
easily swayed. Such was the case in every town. It
would be better for him, and it would look better, if one
of that element managed to catch up with the Trains. It
would be better by far if the Trains did not live long
enough to be brought to justice, for if they had their day
in court Ralston knew that they would have a reasonable
chance of clearing themselves. For those reasons, he
had placed a ten-thousand-dollar bounty on both Mort
and Matt Train. In the eyes of some, at least, it managed
to elevate his position within the community.

Still, he feared the son. Matt Train had a reputation

for his grit and his resiliency. His skills with his fists and his guns were respected. He had no man on his payroll who could best Matt Train. That was the reason he had decided to hedge his bet. He had sent for Lute Kagen, the legendary gunfighter and hired killer. Between Kagen and Ralston's army of thugs, the Trains would be hunted down and killed, or they would be driven out of the territory forever. Their land would be forfeit under the law, and he would become the new owner—a land baron in his own right.

The concept made Ralston burn inside—like bad whiskey taken too fast, slamming hard against one's stomach. He refilled his glass as he smiled to himself and enjoyed his state of complacency.

His mood was shattered when he heard a knock on the door. The knob turned and the door opened. Burl Archer walked in and swung the door shut behind him. He strolled over and stood in front of Ralston's desk, shifting his weight to his left leg while shoving the thumb of his gun hand under his belt. He was about five-ten, one hundred eighty pounds. His shoulders were sloped. He wore a black Stetson and a black shirt that was buttoned at the collar, giving a bulging look to his already thick neck. He wore a beard to conceal the fact that his face was pock-marked.

"What is it?" Ralston asked, a sharp edge to his voice.

Archer shrugged. "Nothin' new. Just reportin' in."

Ralston's disappointment showed on his face. "With all the men we have, why is it we can't find the Trains?"

"Take it easy, Boss. There's plenty of ground to cover out there. If we had ten times the number of men, we might not find 'em. Besides, the Trains know the lay of the land better than anybody. There are ravines, valleys, canyons, mountains . . . why, the U.S. Army might not be able to find 'em if they don't want to be found."

Ralston pushed his shot glass aside. "You still have your men posted?"

Archer nodded. "Every road, the Train ranch house, the assessor's office . . . the usual places. They can hide, but they can't come anywhere near Questor or their homestead without us knowin' about it. That's where we have the advantage over 'em."

Archer made the claim with an assurance that irritated Ralston. He was capable enough with his gun, but he lacked the cunning and the finesse needed to fulfill Ralston's objectives.

"I'm concerned that the Trains may attempt to send in their payment with someone else."

"Not a chance. I've got men in all the right places. Besides, nobody in this town has the sand to try to turn a stunt like that. We've got just about everybody buffaloed."

Ralston said nothing, but he believed that Archer's assessment was accurate.

"Besides, where would they be gettin' the cash to pay their taxes? They can't very well walk into the bank and make a withdrawal—wanted as they are."

Ralston smirked. "They've just delivered a cattle

herd. The sale of their beef would bring enough to pay the taxes of most of the people in this town."

Archer's level of confidence took a dive. Then, he grinned as though something slowly dawned on him. "Yeah, but chances are that the drovers would never get back in time . . . and it wouldn't do 'em any good to wire the money. The Trains can't make an appearance to pick it up."

Ralston secretly agreed with him but he chose not to give Archer the satisfaction. "Maybe . . . maybe not. Either way, a day or two before the tax deadline, send some boys on the road to see if there's any sign of the Train hands. If they're spotted, you know what to do."

Archer's grin widened. "That's what I like about you, Boss. You've got every angle figured. Nothin' slips through your fingers."

"That's why I'm sitting behind this desk making all the decisions. Now, if there's nothing else . . ."

Archer scratched his beard. "Actually, me and the boys ain't been paid yet this week. I was wonderin' if—"

Ralston reached into his desk drawer and pulled out a metal box. Using a key he pulled from his vest pocket, he opened the box and removed a stack of bills, which he tossed on the desk.

Archer reached for the money greedily and crammed it into his pocket. Eyeing the bottle, he licked his lips.

"Pay the men."

"Yes, sir."

"And get yourself a drink."

Archer grinned again as he reached for the bottle. "At the saloon."

The expression on Archer's face changed. He shifted his weight awkwardly from one leg to the other and then turned for the door.

Ralston did not look up again until he heard the door close. Glad that he was alone once again, he reached for the shot glass and poured himself another drink.

Once on the boardwalk, Archer reached into his pocket, counted the bills Ralston had given him, and then separated his share from the rest of the stack. He strolled toward the saloon, pausing to eye a pair of women who crossed the street in front of him. He looked after them until they disappeared into one of the stores on the next block. He then continued on his way, pushing through the batwing doors of the saloon and sidling up to the bar. The establishment was deserted at this hour, save for two men who sat at a table off in one corner. Archer ordered a bottle and then walked over and sat beside them. Zee Martin and Ed Stilson looked at Archer anxiously as he placed the bottle on the table and nodded.

Martin accepted the bottle and quickly filled three glasses. The men drank in silence for a minute, and then Archer dropped some bills in front of them. "Payday, boys," he announced.

Martin and Stilson quickly picked up the money and pocketed it.

"Any new orders?" Martin asked.

"Nope. Just keep on doin' what you've been doin'. You two will cover the Train ranch house tonight. I doubt that anybody will show up, but we've got to keep Ralston happy."

"You figure the Trains have lit out for good?" Stilson queried.

"They'd be mighty foolish if they haven't, what with half the town wantin' to see 'em strung up, and with any gun who's interested in money out after 'em. Either way, when they don't pay their taxes a week from now, Ralston will have won the first round. After that, their land goes up for sheriff's sale, and he'll be able to buy it."

The others chortled.

"Worked out pretty much the way he wanted, didn't it?" Martin put in.

Archer nodded. "As long as we can keep the Trains on the run, Ralston's plan ought to succeed."

Slim Holly's place was about eight miles west of Questor. It was an isolated spot, off the beaten path, and for that reason, Matt Train felt reasonably safe in making an occasional visit while he was on the run. It was a modest layout—a small ranch house, a barn, and the usual outbuildings and corrals. Three horses moseyed about in the largest corral while some chickens scratched in the dirt near the barn. Other than that, there was no activity.

Train and Della sat in their saddles in an arroyo some two hundred yards away. They had held this position for ten minutes as Train scanned the terrain in every direction for signs of anyone. When he felt confident that they were alone, he nodded to Della and they advanced.

When they were about fifty yards from the house, a dog started barking. Seconds later, a man stepped onto the porch, a rifle cradled in his arm. He eyed them suspiciously, but when he recognized Train he smiled and leaned the rifle against the house.

"Howdy, Matt. It's good to see you, boy."

"Hello, Slim."

A bony hound ran up to their horses and started to prance about.

"Get away, Sticks. Go back to sleep in the barn," Slim ordered.

The hound whined for a moment, cast his big eyes about as though temporarily bewildered, and then turned and meandered toward the barn.

Train dismounted and helped Della out of the saddle.

"Who's your pretty friend?" Slim asked.

"Miss Della Dorn, may I present Slim Holly."

"Mr. Holly," Della said with a smile.

"Miss Dorn, it's a pleasure."

"Please call me Della."

"Call me Slim."

Upon closer scrutiny, Della could understand why people referred to him as Slim. He was the thinnest man she had ever seen. He seemed to match his hound dog in appearance. His skin was drawn tightly about his face, accenting his high cheekbones. His neck was long, almost cranelike. His body was built like a fence post, with nothing to lend definition save a wide leather belt with a huge silver buckle.

Slim shook his head. "I don't get it. You're a man on the run, hiding out in the mountains, and you manage to show up on my doorstep with the prettiest gal I've seen in many a year. How do you do it?"

Train grinned. "I wish I could say it's my good looks, but the truth of the matter is that Della here was on the stage when it was waylaid."

"What?"

"Ben Connover was killed."

Slim's expression hardened. "Not Old Ben," he said as he lowered his head. "Was it Apaches?"

Train shook his head. "I figure it was Ralston's doing."

Slim's hands tightened into fists. "Ralston and his coyotes have pushed all the decent folks too far. Why don't the two of us ride into town right now and shoot it out with 'em?"

Train smiled as he placed his hand on Slim's shoulder. "There may come a time when we'll have to do just that, but not yet. There's still a chance to settle this legally— without bloodshed. That was Ben's way, and he died trying to uphold his principles. The least we can do is run out the string—for now anyway."

Slim lowered his head. "I reckon you're right. Gunplay should always be the last resort. That was Ben's way, and it's always been your pa's."

"Yes, it has."

"Well, you two look travel weary. How about something to eat? I've got a batch of biscuits and some beef stew on the stove."

"None for me, Slim. I've left my folks with only one mount, and I want to get back to them as soon as possible. But I'm sure that Della could use some food."

"How about it, Della?"

"No, but thank you, Slim. What I really need is to get to town as soon as possible. My Aunt Marion must be very concerned about me by now."

"Aunt Marion?" Slim mused. "Marion Vale . . . of course. She's a fine lady."

"Thank you," Della said with a smile.

"I'm asking you to take Della into town. This is as far as I can go," Train said.

"You bet I will. I'll take her in on the buckboard. I think she'll be a bit more comfortable, dressed as she is."

"There's one more thing. Della may have some news for me from time to time. It would be convenient if you would serve as our go-between if need be."

Slim brushed his hand across his chin in thought. "Suits me just fine. I don't get much company out here. A pretty face would be mighty welcome."

Train smiled. "By the way, it might not be wise to let anyone know that I was the one who found Della at the stage."

Slim considered him narrowly. "I get your point. Supposin' I just happen to drop the word that I came upon Della, while I was searchin' for strays."

"Sounds good."

Della nodded in agreement.

"I thank you, Slim, and I will take a couple of those biscuits with me."

"Sure enough. I'll have 'em for you in a minute." Slim disappeared into the house.

Turning to Della, Train said, "I'll say good-bye to you now. I'll be leaving you in the best hands I can."

"Thank you for what you've done. I hope that everything works out for you and your family."

She extended her hand, and he took it.

"We probably won't meet again . . . at least not until all this trouble is cleared up."

"I hope it will be soon."

At that, Slim came out of the house carrying a small bundle that he handed to Train.

Train smiled as he stuffed it into his pocket. He swung into his saddle, caught up the horse which Della had ridden, spun Bullwhip and rode off.

"I'll catch up Old Grinder and hitch him to the buckboard, and we'll be on our way," Slim said.

Della nodded. She turned and watched Train as he loped off toward the arroyo. In a matter of minutes, he disappeared from view, leaving only a slight cloud of dust in his wake as the only tangible reminder that he had ever been with her. Della experienced a feeling of sadness welling inside her. It was sympathy, in part, yet she was also woman enough to know that it was something beyond that, a sensation the like of which she had never felt before.

Slim helped Della mount the buckboard, and in no time at all they were jostling along toward town.

For some time neither spoke. Finally, as he regarded Della out of the corner of his eye, Slim ventured, "You kinda' like that boy, don't you?"

Half lost in thought, Della glanced at Slim and blushed.

"No need to feel uncomfortable about it. Most folks like young Matt. He's honest and steady, and he doesn't back down from any man."

"How long have you known him, Slim?"

"By gosh, I was there the day he was born. He had a powerful set of lungs too. His ma and pa and I have been friends for thirty years. There's no finer family, that's for sure."

Della's face furrowed. "This trouble they're in . . . it seems very serious."

"It is that. It all started with a preposterous situation and got fanned like a windstorm by Clegg Ralston and his bunch. Most folks don't believe that Matt or his pa are guilty of anything, but then again, most folks are scared of Ralston. He's got the gullible ones buffaloed. He's created a hornets' nest, and the Trains are caught in the middle of it. Even though the Trains have a clear shot at proving their innocence in court, there's little chance that they'll ever see the likes of a judge. What with Ralston's guns and those greedy no-accounts who are eyein' the reward on the Trains, it's more than likely that they'll be shot on sight."

"Wouldn't it be wiser if they just left the territory for a while—at least until things died down?"

"That's just what Ralston is hoping. He wants to pick up the option on their land once they fail to pay their taxes."

"That's the way the Trains explained the situation to me, but the more I think about it, the more I realize how impossible everything seems to be for them. The land won't do them much good if they're not around to live on it."

"In that case, they'd most likely prefer to die on it."

"What a strange way of looking at things," Della said, looking at him askance.

Aware of how his comment must have sounded to her, Slim took a deep breath and exhaled slowly. "When you've worked the land your whole life, the land becomes a part of you. You live on it, your young 'uns are born on it; when you've run out your string, you expect to be buried on it. It's one of the unwritten codes of the West. A man who won't fight for his land isn't much of a man when it comes down to it." He focused his eyes squarely on Della. "The Trains won't run. They'll do everything they can to clear up this mess peacefully but if they can't, they'll fight. They may get themselves killed in the process but they won't run. You can bet on that."

Marion Vale lived in a small frame house on the outskirts of town. It was pretty, painted light green with white tracery across the front. An inviting porch, girded with white handrails and spindles, ran the entire width of the front of the structure. Some potted plants added a splash of color, and a small garden of mariposa lilies lined the walk.

Slim stopped the buckboard and helped Della step down. As he walked her to the porch, the front door opened and Marion stepped out. She was an attractive woman in her mid-forties. She wore her chestnut-colored hair in a neat bun and held her shoulders in a regal sort of way. She was clad in a sky-blue dress with a lace collar and tiny white buttons. Tears welled in her eyes when she saw Della. Taking her niece in her arms, she squeezed her tightly and whimpered a deep sigh.

"Oh, Della, I was so afraid that the Apaches had carried you away. Are you all right, sweetheart?"

"I'm fine, Aunt Marion. It's wonderful to see you again."

"I wasn't surprised when the stage was late. It happens often, what with broken wheels and all, but this morning the line sent out some riders. They said they found the stage overturned, the driver dead, along with poor Ben Connover, and you missing . . . well, I just didn't know what I was going to do."

"I'm all right, Aunt Marion . . . just a little tired is all. I'll tell you all about it."

"Of course you will." She took Della's face in her hands and kissed her forehead.

"Slim drove me into town from his place."

Turning toward Slim, Marion beamed. "Oh, Slim, thank you ever so much."

"It was my pleasure, Miss Marion. Your niece was the best company I've had in some time."

"Can I offer you something to eat?"

"No, thanks. You and Della have some catchin' up to do. I'll be on my way."

"Oh, Slim, I wonder if you would do me one additional favor? Would you mind telling Mr. Morton at the stage office that you found Della safe and sound and that she's home with me?"

"Why, I'd be glad to."

"I'm sure that he'll have some questions for Della. Tell him that we'll drop by his office first thing in the morning."

"I'll see to it right away, Miss Marion."

"First chance I get, I'll bake an apple pie and take it out to your place."

Slim grinned as he patted his stomach. "Think I can afford the pounds?"

She laughed. "I'd better make it two pies."

Slim climbed onto the buckboard and waved as he pulled away.

Marion and Della wrapped their arms around each other as they walked inside.

"Aunt Marion, I have so much to tell you."

"All in good time, dear. Right now you'll want a bath."

"I guess I do look a sight," Della said, glancing down at her dress.

"I'll heat some water and prepare the tub for you. While you wash, I'll fix supper."

Della nodded.

"Your portmanteau is on the bed in the guest room. A man from the stage line recovered it this morning. At least you'll be able to have a fresh change of clothes."

"That's good news anyway." Della made her way into the bedroom, dropped her handbag on the bed, and quickly removed her clothes. An hour later, she was clean, changed, and seated at her aunt's table. A hearty meal of fried chicken, mashed potatoes and gravy, greens, and steaming hot coffee made her feel human again.

Marion deliberately avoided asking Della for an explanation of her disappearance and her sudden return until she was able to complete her meal in peace. Finally, she said, "Now, tell me everything that happened between the time the stage was attacked and Slim Holly found you."

Della replaced her cup on her saucer and leaned back comfortably in her chair. "Slim didn't find me. Matt Train did."

"Matt Train!" Marion spoke out in surprise. "Why, half the county is out gunning for that poor boy."

"So he told me."

"And he took you to Slim's?"

"Not directly. First, he took me to a hut up in the mountains where I met his folks."

"Sarah and Mortimer!" Marion shook her head in

surprise. "What this community has done to them! Are they all right?"

"Yes, but a little the worse for wear."

"Tell me. Tell me everything."

Della nodded and then proceeded to recount her experience—starting with her struggle with the young Apache, to her encounter with the Trains far back in the mountains, to her journey to Slim Holly's ranch.

Marion listened intently to every word, shaking her head from time to time, aghast at her young niece's narrative. Finally, she breathed a deep sigh of relief. "All I can say is that you're lucky to be alive."

"I guess I was in some danger, all right. Tell me, Aunt Marion, this trouble the Trains are in, is it all as bad as it appears?"

Marion frowned. "I don't see how there's any way out of it for them. Why, there must be fifty people who would gladly shoot them on sight."

"They told me all about it. You believe in them, don't you?"

"Of course I do. I've known Sarah and Mortimer for years. They're good people. And there's no more up-standing man in the territory than Matt. If Matt or his father shot someone, there had to be a just reason. It's just that, somehow, Clegg Ralston has managed to maneuver them into a corner, and now it seems to be too late to get them out."

"This Clegg Ralston must be a bad one."

"He is. Most folks are wise to him, but there is an element in town who see the evidence his way. That, coupled with all the hired guns he has, is enough to keep the Trains on the run."

"I'd like to help him . . . I mean the Trains . . . if I can."

Marion looked at her niece askance. "And just how do you propose to do that, may I ask?"

"I don't know. Maybe I can learn something that might prove important. If I can get close enough to Clegg Ralston—"

"Now, you hold it right there, Della. You're not to go anywhere near Clegg Ralston. He's a dangerous man to run afoul of. Why, we don't even have any real law in this town since Sheriff Marbury was killed. Dub Parker is nothing more than an out-of-work storekeeper appointed by the town council as temporary sheriff—and that was at the urging of Clegg Ralston, who, you can be sure, is lining Parker's pockets. Why, Parker couldn't be entrusted with anything more than jailing drunks on Saturday night."

"I promise that I won't have any direct contact with Ralston or any of his men, but that doesn't mean that I can't pick up any useful information while I'm in town. If there's anything I learn that might prove to be of use to Matt and his family, there's no reason why I can't share that information with them."

Marion regarded her niece closely, a twinkle forming in her eye.

Della flushed under her aunt's scrutiny. She broke eye contact by lifting her cup to her lips.

"And how would you go about getting information to him . . . I mean, to the Trains?"

"We agreed that I could pass it to them through Slim Holly."

"Oh, then you've already agreed to such a plan?"

"Well, yes."

Marion considered Della's response for a long while. "Well, I suppose that such an arrangement could work. If it could help Sarah and Mortimer in any way, I'm certainly for it. You can count on me," she said as she placed her hands on the table decisively. "Besides, I promised Slim some apple pie, so I'll be riding out to his place in a day or two anyway. The two of us could go together . . . that is, unless you think I'd be in the way."

Della grinned at her aunt.

Chapter Four

Snake Danford came upon the camp by chance. There was a small fire at the entrance to a cave. Three horses were picketed nearby. He worked his way through some rocks, maneuvering himself into a position some fifty feet from the mouth of the cave. From here, he could see the glow from the flames casting shadows against the interior walls. A saddle rested inside, and a blanket roll lay beside it. Danford remained hidden for some time, waiting for any movement or sign, but he neither saw nor heard anything. Danford gambled that Matt Train and his mother and father were inside. The three horses suggested exactly that. Of course, it could be three hunters, or some travelers simply passing through the mountains. Danford shrugged off such a possibility. If he were wrong, he would bury his mistakes, and no one would be

63

the wiser. There was too much money on the table to worry about details. Besides, he could always ride away with the horses. They would bring a respectable price.

Danford raised his shotgun. It was the tool of his trade. Its use required neither speed nor accuracy; its only restriction was proximity. That mattered little to Danford, who never met his prey face to face. His style was to approach his mark through stealth, by crawling on his belly or hiding behind rocks or brush. He leveled the barrel at the bedroll and squeezed the trigger. A deafening shot rang out, shattering the stillness of the night. The horses lurched, whinnying at the sound of the shotgun. There was no movement or sound from the cave. Danford knew that he had hit his target. There were two left, and he reasoned that he had them covered. He could wait them out or go in firing. It would be like shooting fish in a barrel.

"Come on out, you Trains. You're trapped, and there's no place to go!" Danford called out.

There was no response. Only the horses shuffled their feet uneasily.

Cautiously, Danford rose to his feet. He stepped around the rock and edged toward the cave. When he was halfway there, he heard a clicking sound behind him. He recognized it at once as the cocking of a gun. Danford froze in his tracks.

"It just so happens that this cave has two entrances, Danford," a voice announced coldly. "Drop the shotgun and raise your hands."

Danford licked his lips as a nervous smile twisted his face. Slowly, he turned his head. He saw Train standing just behind him, a .45 in his hand. "Train . . . Matt Train," Danford said, almost in disbelief.

"You called it, bounty hunter."

"Look, it's nothin' personal. It's just . . . business."

"I don't like the way you conduct business."

"Supposin' I just throw down my gun and ride out of here. We'll just forget all about this."

"Why don't you start by throwing down your gun."

"Sure, Train, sure . . . only, don't shoot." Danford held his shotgun at arm's length, but instead of dropping it, he dropped to the ground and rolled. When he came to his knees, he had the shotgun leveled on Train.

Train fired first, and Danford cried out in pain as he discharged the second barrel into the air and fell over backward.

Train moved forward and kicked the shotgun away from Danford. He removed the handgun from Danford's holster and tucked it under his own belt.

"You hurt me, Train, you hurt me bad," Danford moaned as he squirmed on the ground.

Train knelt down and turned Danford over onto his back.

The bounty hunter cried out in pain.

"You've got a bullet in your shoulder, but you'll live."

"I'll bleed to death. I need a doctor . . . bad," he uttered through gritted teeth.

"There's a doctor in Questor. You'll have to make it."

"I'll never make it. I'll bleed to death in these mountains."

"You've left plenty of men to bleed to death in your wake, Danford."

"Please, Train, don't leave me out here to die." He clenched his fists in pain.

"Stop whining. You'll only aggravate the wound . . . and me," Train said as he ripped the sleeve from Danford's shirt.

Thirty minutes later, Train had successfully stopped the bleeding in Danford's shoulder, bandaged him, and fashioned a sling. He located the bounty hunter's horse tied in a thicket about a hundred yards away and put him in the saddle.

"You're not goin' to turn me out without a gun?" Danford asked in alarm.

"That's right. I don't want you doubling back on me and putting a bullet in me from ambush."

"You can't leave me alone in this country without a gun. There are Apaches out here."

Train grinned. He slapped the horse's rump, and the animal lurched forward.

Danford cried out in pain. "Train!" he called out over his shoulder. "Train . . . the Apaches will get me. I'm in no shape to fight or run. Train!"

Della awoke early the next morning, rested and refreshed. She heard her aunt bustling about in the kitchen, and she soon detected the aroma of fresh baked biscuits, bacon, and coffee. She sat on the edge of the bed and stretched her arms, still feeling a bit tender in her shoulder and halfway down her rib cage from the stage mishap. Even so, she concluded that she felt better and climbed out of bed.

Marion was in her apron, moving about her tiny kitchen with an economy of movement that always astonished Della.

"Good morning, dear. Did you sleep well?" her aunt asked as she placed a creamer and some utensils on the white table cloth.

"Yes, I was very tired."

"I should imagine. Once you get some food inside of you, you'll feel even better."

"It smells delicious."

"Well, after all, your mother taught me how to cook, bless her soul," Marion said over her shoulder.

Her Aunt Marion resembled her mother in many ways—not only in her physical features but also in the way she carried herself. Maybe that was one reason why Della had always looked forward to visiting her aunt. It brought her mother back in a way.

"Yes, Mother was a splendid cook. I miss her every day," Della said with an edge of sadness.

Marion turned away for a moment, a tear forming in her eye. She placed a dish of scrambled eggs and three strips of bacon before Della. Next, she filled Della's cup with steaming coffee. She then prepared a setting for herself and sat down across the table from Della.

"What are your plans for today, Aunt Marion?" Della asked as she placed a pat of butter on a hot biscuit.

"It's Saturday, and I have to work in the shop."

"Oh, I'd love to help you as I did the last time I was here."

"That would be wonderful, but I think it might be wise if you rested for a spell. You've been through quite an ordeal."

"Oh, I'm fine. Besides, I want to get a feel for the town, and I'm sure that there must be plenty of your customers who are brimming with useful information."

Marion winked at her. "Gossip, you mean. Yes, we have our share of tattlers. In fact, there's probably no better place in Questor for the latest news among ladies than the milliner's shop. I guess it's just a natural thing—like men congregating around a barber shop or in the saloon."

"Now, there's an idea. I'll bet if I could spend a little time in the saloon—"

"Della, please! You're positively scandalous."

They both enjoyed a good laugh.

"Truthfully, Aunt Marion, I would like to go to the shop with you."

Marion took a sip from her cup. "All right, I suppose if you feel up to it, but remember . . . we need to stop in at the stage line office first."

"I remember."

"Now, you'd better get your story straight before we speak to Mr. Morton."

Mr. Morton was a short, stocky man of about sixty. He wore a brown corduroy coat, a shoestring tie, and a shiny silver belt buckle. His gray mustache matched his wavy hair in color and texture. He stood up in a gentlemanly fashion as Marion and Della entered his office. After he seated them, he resumed his position behind a scarred walnut desk that was littered with papers.

"Slim Holly dropped by yesterday to tell me that he delivered you safely into town, Miss Dorn. Speaking on behalf of the stage line, I can't begin to tell you how relieved I am that you were not lost with the driver and the other passenger. It must have been a harrowing experience for you."

"It was, to say the least, Mr. Morton," Della returned.

"I can assure you that this has been the first instance of trouble we've had in over a year. The stage line takes pride in the service it provides its customers."

Della nodded.

"The Apaches can be an unpredictable breed but as I've explained, they haven't been this bold in some time."

"It wasn't Apaches who attacked the stage, Mr. Morton."

His jaw dropped in surprise as he leaned back in his chair. "What? But we found tracks of unshod ponies at the site of the stage wreck."

"Oh, there was an Apache there all right—a young buck, who gave me some rather anxious moments, but he came after the stage had been attacked . . . by white men."

"Are you sure?"

Della nodded.

"Can you identify any of them?"

"I'm afraid not."

Mr. Morton took a deep breath and let it out slowly. He placed his hands on the desk before him and focused closely on Della. "Suppose you tell me exactly what happened—from the beginning."

Della proceeded to relate everything that had transpired, omitting her encounter with the Trains, claiming instead that Slim Holly had found her and brought her into town.

Mr. Morton listened intently. When Della concluded her narrative, he was obviously upset.

"My dear, I'm stunned with disbelief. Why, that stage wasn't carrying a strongbox. We didn't even have a man riding shotgun."

"Perhaps they were after something else." As soon as she had made the remark, Della regretted it. Out of the corner of her eye, she could see her aunt regarding her narrowly.

Mr. Morton considered her closely. Finally, he said, "Perhaps. I'll inform Sheriff Parker of your story. He may want to question you further. Thank you for coming in, and I can promise you that the next time you travel on this line, your ride will be paid for."

"That's very kind of you, sir."

Della and Marion rose to their feet.

Mr. Morton opened the door and ushered them out.

Once outside on the boardwalk, Marion turned to Della. "That was close. I thought for sure that last remark was going to get you into something that you couldn't get out of. Luckily, you were vague enough to suggest something without having to furnish an explanation for it."

"It can't hurt to make people think. Maybe if people think this matter through a little bit more, they will recognize exactly what's going on in this town."

"I think there's more to it than that, Della. Most folks here are good people. It's one thing what they believe; it's another what they can do about it. The residents of Questor are storekeepers, farmers, and ranchers. They're not gunmen."

"That's exactly what the Trains said, and I appreciate that, but we can't stand by and do nothing while the Trains are destroyed by the likes of Clegg Ralston and his . . . his . . ."

"Coyotes?"

"Yes . . . coyotes. That's exactly what Slim Holly called them."

"Slim Holly refers to most people as coyotes."

They smiled at each other and continued along the boardwalk until they reached Marion's millinery shop. Marion took a key from her handbag and unlocked the door.

As they entered, Della glanced about the room and beamed. "Oh, Aunt Marion, it's beautiful! You've done so many wonderful things since I was here last."

"Oh, a little paint and a few decorations, nothing more."

"It's a marvelous little shop."

Marion gave Della a tour, pointing out the location of the wares she sold and how best to dispense them. There were hats of all shapes, sizes, and designs. Bolts of material lined shelves. Ribbons, lace, thread, needles, thimbles, and other such notions were neatly arranged and displayed.

It was not long before an elderly lady arrived, whom Marion introduced as Mrs. Ginger. Marion greeted her warmly, and the three ladies chatted for some time. Mrs. Ginger asked many questions of Della—about St. Louis, the fashions in her part of the country, and a number of similar topics. She seemed to examine every article in the shop but left with only ten cents worth of green ribbon.

Marion uttered a deep sigh. "Mrs. Ginger is nice enough, but like so many other customers, she doesn't buy enough to keep me in business. I've had to take up a little dressmaking to earn extra money. Come on, I'll show you the back room where I do the fittings." She hesitated, however, as she neared the front window. "It didn't take long for Mr. Morton to speak to Dub Parker. He's coming over right now."

Della looked out the window and saw two men approaching. "Which one is he?"

"The short one in the wine-colored shirt."

"Who's the man with him?"

"Cord Renfro. He's one of Clegg Ralston's hired guns."

"He's wearing a badge."

"Ralston finagled it so that Renfro could work as Parker's deputy. That way, he can do pretty much what he wants, and it's legal."

"He looks familiar somehow."

"I doubt that you've ever seen him before. He came to town with Ralston. That was long after your last visit."

Della eyed Renfro closely and wondered.

The two men entered the shop and stood before Marion. Parker tipped his Stetson. He was about forty-five, slight in stature, and sallow of complexion. Renfro was taller and thicker through the chest. He wore a black Stetson with a high crown. His nose looked as though it had been broken at some time, and he carried a curved scar just above his nose and across his forehead.

"Mornin', Miss Marion."

"Good morning, Dub. What can I do for you?"

"Actually, I came to interview your niece concerning the attack on the stage. Mr. Morton just gave me his report on the matter."

"Well, this is my niece, Della Dorn. Della, this is Dub Parker, acting sheriff of Questor."

Della nodded.

"Miss Della," Parker said, nodding his head. "This is my deputy, Cord Renfro."

Della looked at Renfro, but he did not speak, nor did he alter his expression. He merely eyed Della with a scrutiny that made her uncomfortable.

"Miss Della, Mr. Morton told me about your experience on the stage."

"Yes, it was dreadful."

"I'm sure it was. He tells me that it wasn't Apaches that attacked the stage, but white men."

"That's correct."

"Yet you couldn't identify any of 'em."

"No, I'm afraid I didn't see them."

Parker pushed back his Stetson. "Well, miss, if you didn't see 'em, then just how did you know they were white men?"

Renfro regarded her closely.

Marion shifted her weight uneasily from one foot to the other.

Della's lips twitched uneasily. "It was because of something that the other passenger said—Mr. Connover, I believe his name was. The poor man."

"Yes?"

"Well, when the stage was attacked, Mr. Connover told me to get down on the floor. I did as he instructed."

"Then, you didn't actually see anybody?"

"No, but Mr. Connover said, quite distinctly, that we were being attacked by bandits. He wouldn't have used that term if they would have been Apaches, would he?"

Parker rubbed his hand across his chin. "No, I guess he wouldn't."

"Then, when the stage overturned, I must have struck my head. When I came to . . . it could have been hours later . . . I was alone. Mr. Connover and the driver were dead. Oh, it's true, there was a young Apache rummaging about, and he put quite a scare in me, but when Slim Holly arrived on the scene, he ran off."

"I see. That's a long way from Slim Holly's spread. I wonder what he was doin' that far off?"

"I'm sure I don't know, Sheriff. I wasn't in any condition to ask."

Parker and Renfro exchanged looks.

"Is there anything else you'd like to ask, Dub?" Marion said.

"No, ma'am, I guess not." Turning to Della, he said, "You'll be in town for a while?"

"Yes, I will. I'm planning to stay on with my aunt for a few weeks."

"If I need you, then I'll know where to find you." He touched the brim of his Stetson and turned for the door.

Renfro passed his fingers through some lace in the window display, ran his eyes over Della one more time, and then followed Parker out onto the street.

"He's a cold one," Della said, shivering.

Marion placed her arm around Della and nodded. "I didn't like the way he looked at you. I wonder if it's going to be safe for you to remain here in Questor?"

Della touched her cheek and felt herself trembling. She glanced in the direction of the cheval mirror Marion used for fittings and discovered that she was pale. She moved to the counter and picked up her handbag. She opened it and removed her hand mirror, with which she examined her complexion more closely.

"What is it, Della? Are you all right?"

Della did not respond. She merely stared at her hand mirror as if in a trance.

"Della! Are you ill?"

"That's it, Aunt Marion. I remember now."

"Remember what?"

"Where I saw Cord Renfro before."

Marion approached the counter and faced Della.

"It was when I was on the stage. He was one of the men who attacked it and killed Mr. Connover and the driver."

"Are you sure?" Marion asked, stunned.

Della nodded.

"But you said that you didn't see any of the men who attacked the stage."

"And so I did . . . but I was wrong. I must have been in and out of consciousness after the stage overturned. When I came to, my handbag was on the floor, and my mirror lay beside it. The mirror was only a few inches from my face as I lay on the floor of the stage. I could barely open my eyes, but I recall now looking into the mirror and seeing the reflection of a face peering in, staring at me for a long time. It was the face of a man. He was wearing a mask, but there was no mistaking those eyes and that scar across his forehead. It was Cord Renfro. He must have thought that I was dead or that I would never be able to recognize him and the others. That's why he left me as I was. I thought the whole thing was a bad dream—you know, the kind you have sometimes when you're sick—but when I saw him again just now, it all started to come back to me, and then, when I looked into the mirror . . . well, it all became real again."

"Sometimes when you suffer a blow to the head or a shock to your system, you block things out of your memory."

"That must have been the case."

"And that must have been the reason why Renfro eyed you so narrowly. He must have been surprised to see you. And that means that you're in danger. Renfro could return at any time and try to kill you if he changes his mind and thinks that you could identify him."

Della frowned as she placed the mirror on the counter and looked more closely into her handbag. She reached in and removed some folded sheets of paper. Puzzled, she glanced at Marion and then placed the papers on the counter. Marion moved closer and peered over Della's shoulder as her niece unfolded the papers and smoothed them out.

"Where did these come from?" Della mused.

"What are they?"

"I don't know. I've never seen them before."

Marion leaned closer. "They're official looking documents. Why, the name BENJAMIN CONNOVER, ATTORNEY AT LAW is inscribed on the top. How did they come to be in your handbag?"

Della and Marion regarded each other closely.

"Mr. Connover must have concealed these papers in my handbag after the stage overturned . . . when I was unconscious. This is what the men who attacked the stage must have been after. I had them all the time. When I came to, I dropped my hand mirror back into my bag, but I didn't really look inside. This is the first time I've opened it since."

For the next several minutes the women pored over the documents, so engrossed in what it was they were reading that they did not even speak. Finally, Marion exhaled deeply, not realizing that she must have been holding her breath.

"According to this, Clegg Ralston's real name is Eliot Brandon, and he's wanted in Denver for questioning in a man's murder."

"And this paper says that a man named Webb Crane is residing in a hotel in a town called Clayton. It says that he's using the name Hastings."

"Clayton is a small town to the north, about forty-five miles from here."

"Webb Crane . . . I believe I recall the Trains mentioning that name."

Marion nodded. "Webb Crane was a witness against the Trains in the shootings of Sheriff Marbury and his deputy. He disappeared shortly afterward. Most folks are of the opinion that he was dead, along with another witness, Steve Payton."

"Then this Webb Crane can clear the Trains if he can be persuaded to tell the truth," Della ventured.

"He could. He's the only one who isn't one of Ralston's gunmen who was present at the shootings." Marion paused. "We have to get this information to the law."

"But what law, Aunt Marion? Certainly not Dub Parker."

"No, that wouldn't do."

"The Trains mentioned a U.S. marshal named Weldon."

"Yes, Frank Weldon from Warrensburg. It would be best if we could get it to him. He's the only honest authority here about. With this information, Ralston could be discredited and the Trains could be cleared."

"But how can we get it to him?"

"That's a good question. Warrensburg is a long way from here. We certainly can't trust the stage, and we could never make a ride like that."

"Why couldn't we wire the marshal that we have important information for him?"

"Because Ralston will have the telegraph covered. That would bring him to our doorstep faster than taking out an ad in the newspaper."

Della considered the matter for a long moment. "Then we'll have to get the documents to Slim Holly. He's the only direct contact we have with Matt Train. We agreed that I could pass information on to him through Slim. It will be up to Matt to pick up the documents. It will be up to Matt and his folks to determine what to do with them.

After all, the documents rightly belong to the Trains. It was their lawyer who obtained this information, and he died trying to get it to them."

Marion eyed Della closely. Finally, she nodded. "I don't see any other practical way. It looks as though I'm going to be baking those apple pies for Slim sooner than I expected."

Chapter Five

Clegg Ralston rolled his cheroot slowly between his fingers as he eyed Cord Renfro through a cloud of smoke. "You told me the girl was dead."

"I thought she was," Renfro returned, a defensive edge in his voice.

"You're certain she can't identify you?"

"Dead certain. She never even looked at me. She must have been knocked unconscious."

Ralston placed the cheroot between his lips and inhaled. His eyes became slits as he blew smoke out of the side of his mouth. "How did she react when she saw you in the millinery?"

"She didn't. She showed no signs of recognizing me at all. I'm convinced the story she told was the truth."

Ralston considered Renfro for a long time. "Keep an

81

eye on her for the next few days. If you discover that she's lying, you know what to do."

Renfro nodded. "Danford's still at Doc Harrigan's. Looks like Train shot him up pretty bad."

"The fool. Danford's lucky to be alive, tangling with the likes of Matt Train."

"Are you goin' to talk to him?"

"I'll give the doc time to finish patching him up. Then I'll go see him."

"Right." Renfro left Ralston's office wearing a smug expression, knowing that he was going to enjoy his next job. There was nothing he wanted to do more than to watch Della Dorn. He strolled down the boardwalk until he reached the mercantile, where he took a seat on a wooden bench. From this position, he could observe the millinery without being noticed himself.

Snake Danford winced in pain as Doc Harrigan tied the final knot into his bandage. "Go easy, will you, Doc? I ain't no sack of grain."

"You should stay in bed for the next few days, and don't try to lift anything with that arm," Harrigan said as he assessed his work.

"Now, what would I be liftin'? With the way this shoulder feels, I'll be lucky if I can pick up a fork, let alone a .45."

"Oh, you'll be all right in a week or so. It's not as bad as you think."

Danford grimaced as he considered Harrigan. "If it wasn't for Matt Train, I'd—"

"If it weren't for Matt Train patching you up the way he did, you most likely would have bled to death. Now, just lie back against that pillow and rest for a while. I'll see about getting you some broth."

"Broth? What I need is a stiff shot of rye."

"No alcohol. You need to be on a simple and basic diet for a while. Now, stop squirming and stay quiet. I don't want that wound to open up."

Harrigan washed his hands and toweled them dry. He looked in the mirror. His hair was gray now and there were heavy lines on his face. Suddenly, he felt very weary. He left his operating room and returned to his front office, where he saw Clegg Ralston sitting in one of the chairs. He neither liked nor trusted Ralston. Furthermore, he believed that the recent trouble Questor had experienced had been Ralston's doing.

"Mornin', Doc. How's your patient?"

"He'll live," Harrigan replied coldly.

"Glad to hear it. Any reason why I can't see him for a few minutes?"

"I suppose not but keep it brief."

Ralston nodded. He walked into the operating room, where he saw Danford stretched out on the bed, his arm and shoulder heavily bandaged.

"How are you feeling, Snake?"

Danford opened his eyes and focused on Ralston.

"Oh, Mr. Ralston, I'm . . . all right, I guess. At least, that's what that butcher tells me."

"I heard that it was Matt Train that did this to you."

"You heard right enough. If he would've faced me, man to man, instead of comin' up behind me, his body would be slung over a saddle now, and I'd be collectin' that reward you offered."

Ralston sneered at Danford's remark. "Just where was it that this shoot-out took place?"

"About half a day's ride west." Danford described the location of the cave and its surroundings.

Ralston listened closely to Danford's words. "He's still in the territory, then," he said, half to himself.

"He's still around."

"Was he alone?"

"He appeared to be. There were three horses in his camp but I didn't see anybody else."

Ralston nodded. He reached into his pocket and pulled out a cheroot, which he handed to Danford. "When you're on your feet again, look me up."

When Ralston was on the boardwalk again in front of Doc Harrigan's office, he paused and looked up and down the street.

Archer stepped up to him. "Anything new on Train?"

"No. According to Danford, he was most likely alone."

"Do you want me and some of the boys to ride out to where Danford last saw him? Maybe we can pick up his trail."

"It wouldn't do any good. Train's too smart to linger

around the area. He's miles away by now, and he knows how to travel without leaving any sign."

"We don't have anything to lose by tryin'."

"Only more men. Train and his father know those mountains better than the Apaches. They can stay hidden as long as they want to, and they could pick you off one by one."

Archer nodded as he scratched the stubble on his chin. "I reckon you're right but they can't hurt us as long as they're in hiding, and they sure as rain can't come near town."

"That's true enough. I have to admit, though, I'm a little surprised that they're still in the area, and it's got me worried."

Marion and Della agreed that they would visit Slim Holly the next afternoon, following church services. They concluded that it would serve little purpose in going immediately. Despite the importance of the documents Della had found, it was unlikely that Matt Train would return to Slim's place for several days. Besides, if they were being watched, as Marion suspected they might be, a sudden visit to Slim's might arouse suspicion. For the remainder of the day, they decided to go on about their business as planned.

Marion had an appointment for lunch with a friend named Edna Hamilton, and she invited Della to attend. Della eagerly accepted, and they walked together to the hotel restaurant. Miss Hamilton was a polite, friendly lady who wore her gray hair in a tidy bun. She had tiny spectacles that enhanced her large brown eyes, which seemed to notice everyone and everything. She was very gracious to Della, showing what Della took to be a genuine interest in her. The three of them talked on and on as they enjoyed a tasty meal.

Della liked the restaurant. It was clean and neat and very well managed. It also appeared to be a major attraction to the town residents, for nearly every table was occupied, and the patrons were obviously satisfied with the food and the service. After a time, there was some commotion on the far side of the dining room. Della looked up when she heard it. A new arrival was shaking hands with some patrons who appeared to be businessmen. Some laughing and backslapping drew the attention of everyone in the room. The one who had just entered—a tall, nice looking man in his mid-thirties—seemed to be on the receiving end of some congratulations.

Noticing that the incident had caught her niece's attention, Marion said, "Oh, that's Charles Ames, the lawyer. Isn't he handsome?"

"Yes, he is."

"And he's also very successful. He just won an important case for Mr. Woodley—that man in the dark suit," Miss Hamilton added.

"He came to Questor about six months ago—from New York," Marion said. "He hung up his shingle, and he's doing quite well for himself."

"He's very personable," Miss Hamilton put in. "If I were thirty years younger . . ."

They all laughed.

When Ames finished talking, he made his way across the dining room. Seeing Miss Hamilton wave, he detoured to their table.

"Good afternoon, ladies."

"Good afternoon, Mr. Ames," Miss Hamilton chimed.

"Mr. Ames, I'd like you to meet my niece Della from St. Louis."

"How do you do?" he asked, eyeing Della with interest.

"I'm very well, thank you. It's nice to meet you, Mr. Ames." Della noticed that he had wavy brown hair, finely chiseled features, and a warm smile.

"Please call me Charles."

Miss Hamilton winked at Marion.

"I heard about your trouble on the stage," Ames remarked.

"Word certainly gets around fast," Della replied.

"Well, Questor is a small town. You'll find the lifestyle here considerably different from that of St. Louis. Besides, being an attorney, well . . . I have to keep my eyes and ears open . . . as I'm sure you understand."

"Of course."

"May I join you ladies?"

Marion glanced at Miss Hamilton. "Well, I did promise to do a fitting for Miss Hamilton, but Della can stay and chat with you if she likes."

Della suddenly felt awkward. "Well, I—"

"Oh, please, Della. I see that you've already eaten, but perhaps you could have another cup of coffee with me before you leave. We could get to know each other."

Della smiled. "That would be nice."

Ames pulled out the chairs for Marion and Miss Hamilton.

"I'll see you back at the shop shortly, Della," Marion said.

"Fine, Aunt Marion."

Ames dropped his hat on one of the empty chairs and pulled up another one. "Your aunt told me that she had an attractive niece, but she certainly underestimated your charms."

Della smiled. "You're very kind."

"Not at all. What is it that you do in St. Louis, Della?"

"I work on a weekly newspaper. It was owned by my father and his partner. My father passed away earlier this year, and I've stayed on, but I haven't decided yet if it's what I want to do on a permanent basis."

"A fine profession. We could use new blood like you in Questor. The West is a gold mine for those who are willing to exploit it."

"Exploit it?"

He laughed. "Perhaps that isn't the best choice of words. 'Take advantage' of it would be more appropriate."

Della nodded her understanding.

"I'm only sorry that your visit to Questor was marred by the stagecoach incident. I was surprised to learn that the Apaches were't involved."

"Oh, there were Apaches there, all right—or, at least, one of them. A young warrior gave me a hard time until"—Della bit her tongue—"until Slim Holly happened along. I don't know what I would have done if it hadn't been for him."

"But it wasn't the Apaches who attacked the stage?"

"No. They were white men."

"Could you recognize any of them?"

"No. As I told the sheriff, I must have been unconscious by the time they came close enough. The stage overturned, you know."

"Yes."

The waitress approached the table and refilled Della's cup. She filled one for Ames and then took his order.

"I don't suppose you've heard anything about the trouble we've had involving the Train family?"

As Della took a sip of her coffee, she thought that she detected Ames regarding her narrowly. "I believe my aunt mentioned something about it. It seems to be big news around here."

"The biggest news that ever hit these parts. We lost our judge, sheriff, and deputy because of the Trains."

"My aunt is of a different opinion. She believes the Trains are law-abiding citizens."

Ames smiled. "There is an element in town that shares

that feeling. I, for one, do not. As an attorney, I would have to say that the evidence against them is highly damaging."

"Then, you wouldn't be likely to take up their defense?"

"Della, a good attorney can institute a defense for any client, but an ambitious one has to choose his cases carefully."

"What do you mean?"

Ames took a sip of his coffee. "At present, the prevailing winds are blowing against the Trains."

Della nodded.

"The most influential man in the territory at the moment is Clegg Ralston. It's my opinion that the future of Questor—of the territory—rests in his hands."

"I take it then that you mean it would be unwise to do anything that might oppose Mr. Ralston?"

"Della, it would be political suicide."

Della listened for some time as Ames discussed the state of the town of Questor, the future of the territory, and his status within the community. Finally, after a respectable period, Della excused herself by explaining that she should return to the millinery.

Ames stood up. "I hope I can see you again, Della."

"I hope so, too, Charles."

"Perhaps if you're free . . . Monday evening, we can have dinner?"

"That would be nice."

"May I call on you?"

"Yes."

He pulled out her chair, and she left the restaurant.

Della thought about Charles Ames as she made her way back to the millinery. She found her aunt alone in the shop.

"Isn't he a charming man?" Marion asked, approaching her.

"He certainly is."

"He seemed to be attracted to you."

Della shrugged.

"Well, tell me all about it. How did things go?"

"They went just fine, Aunt Marion. He asked me to dinner Monday evening."

Marion beamed. "Why, that's wonderful! Mr. Ames is one of the up-and-coming members of the community."

Della half smiled.

"Why, what's wrong?"

"I don't know exactly—just a feeling, I suppose."

"What do you mean?"

"Well, I had the strangest sensation that he was more interested in what I knew than in me."

"How so?"

Della faced her aunt. "He knew exactly what I told Dub Parker this morning. Ames had to have spoken to him about the stage in order to have known what I said."

"Well, maybe he did. He's curious, just like everyone else in town. When there's an event like a stage robbery, it's important news."

"Yes, but he asked me almost the same exact questions that Dub Parker asked. It was as though he was trying to trap me into saying something different."

"Maybe that's just the lawyer in him coming out."

"Maybe. I don't know, but I nearly slipped and mentioned that it was Matt Train that came upon the stage instead of Slim Holly."

"Oh, Della, be careful."

"Don't worry. I will."

Following his lunch with Della, Ames returned to his office. He had half of the bottom floor of a building owned by Ralston, the other half being the office of the town dentist. Ames walked through the outer office, which was normally occupied by his secretary, a middle-aged spinster who was presently out of town visiting her mother. He strolled into his private office, hung his hat on a tree, and moved behind his desk. It was a reasonably nice arrangement—shelves lined with law books, a diploma on one wall, a nice leather settee, some wing chairs, and his large, highly polished desk, made of walnut. It was neatly kept—a pen and ink set, some papers bearing official seals, and a single lamp with a green shade. Ames settled comfortably into his high-backed, padded chair and stared out the only window in the room at the activity on the street.

For several minutes, he just watched the people as they walked by on the boardwalk or rode past on horseback or in wagons. It was a nice town, he thought—a town with potential. He could become a big man here—an important man if he played his cards close to the vest. Already, he was held in high regard here. He had made connections, significant connections. He could ill afford to jeopardize his status by committing an error in judgement.

Ames reflected upon his past. It had been a little over a year ago when he had left New York under a cloud. He had managed to keep that part of his life hidden. That was the reason he had come west. Here, he believed he could lose himself in the vastness of the land. Here, a man was judged on his merit—not for his past. It was true that his past had been marred by his own foolishness and his greed. He had wanted too much, too soon. He had taken advantage of an elderly client of the firm for which he worked. It had been over a relatively small sum of money, $3,000, yet it was an unprincipled act. The members of his firm discovered it. The money was returned; there was talk of disbarment. Heated words were exchanged. A public scandal was avoided, however, and he was asked to resign.

Questor had given him new life. His connection with Ralston had proven to be a sound one. He had read Ralston's intent to overthrow the Train family, and he believed that Ralston would succeed. Scruples aside, he reasoned that it was smart to back Ralston. If things worked out, he could emerge as the attorney for one of the wealthiest men in the territory. On the other hand, if Ralston were to fall, Ames could still distance himself so that he would be in the clear, at least from a legal standpoint. It would be tantamount to betting on a losing horse. Ames would be a little lighter in the pocket but he could still walk away from the track—if he played by the rules. It was true that he was walking a fine line. He had to position himself so that he could work with Ralston while, at the same time, he could not allow himself to be drawn too deeply into Ralston's circle. It was a delicate balance that he had to maintain. If he acquitted himself well, he could take home a tidy profit without getting tarnished.

His concentration was broken when he heard a knock at his rear door. He turned to see Ralston enter. Ames immediately stood up.

"Mr. Ralston, please sit down."

Ralston took a seat in one of the wing chairs. He casually lit one of his cheroots and blew a cloud of smoke into the air.

Ames resumed his seat and looked at Ralston intently.

"I understand you talked to the girl."

Ames nodded.

"Well?"

"I don't know."

"What do you mean you don't know?"

"She seems to be genuine enough, but there was one moment in our conversation when she hesitated. In my line of work, you train yourself so that you're able to read a person well. I thought I detected a glimmer of something that she may have been concealing. Of course,

I could be wrong. The girl was in an accident. She suffered a blow to the head. She was tired. It's a little too soon to tell."

Ralston regarded Ames closely as he puffed on his cheroot in silence. "You're going to see her again?"

"Yes, I've asked her to dinner."

"Good. If she knows more than she's letting on, I want to hear about it."

"I'll do what I can, Mr. Ralston."

"You'll do more than that. There's too much at stake for us to fail. I want nothing left to chance. Remember, you're sitting behind that desk because I put you there. You're the number one lawyer in Questor now that I've taken out Ben Connover, and I don't expect you to forget that fact."

"I can assure you that I won't, Mr. Ralston. I won't let you down."

"I'm sure you won't. Those who disappoint me aren't around very long."

Ames suddenly felt uneasy as Ralston scrutinized him through a thick cloud of smoke.

When Ralston stood up, Ames rose immediately. He made an effort to give Ralston a reassuring nod and watched with rising uncertainty as Ralston left. Ames swallowed hard as he stared at the door Ralston had closed behind him. He suddenly realized that he was in a box now. Because he had attached himself to Ralston, he no longer controlled his own destiny. He was now taking orders from another. That, in itself, was not necessarily a bad thing, but for the first time in his dealings with Ralston, he felt physically threatened. He was mired deep in the biggest game of his life, and the stakes appeared to be higher than he was willing to concede. It was only a short while ago that he had felt comfortable, even complacent. All at once, his mouth felt dry, and his hands began to shake. Turning back to his desk, he opened a drawer and removed a bottle. He poured himself a drink and swallowed it quickly as he contemplated his vulnerability.

Doc Harrigan limped down the boardwalk on his way to the stable. He was about to make his rounds at a few of the ranches outside of town. Before leaving, however, he stopped by the millinery to see Marion Vale.

Marion greeted him warmly as he entered and placed his medical bag on the counter. "Oh, Doc, I'd like you to meet my niece Della from St. Louis."

Harrigan smiled. "Welcome to Questor, Della."

"Hello, Doc, and thank you."

"Your aunt has been looking forward to your visit for some time now."

"It's good to see her again."

"I expected that Marion would have brought you over to the office following your close call on the stage, but you don't seem to be in need of any medical attention."

"No, I'm feeling fine . . . a little sore is all."

"Well, sometimes injuries don't show up until days later. If that happens, don't hesitate to call on me."

"I won't."

"Maybe the three of us can get together for dinner some evening before you return to St. Louis," Harrigan suggested.

"I'd look forward to that," Marion replied.

"So would I," Della added, smiling.

Harrigan's expression turned serious. "By the way, Marion, I've got Snake Danford in my office."

At the mention of the name, Della bristled.

"Snake Danford! What's he doing in town?" Marion asked.

"Trying to earn a dollar—in his usual way."

"He's after the Trains, no doubt."

"He was but not any more."

Della's eyes widened with fear. "What do you mean?" she asked.

"He caught up with Matt Train, or I should say that Matt Train caught up with him. Matt put a bullet in Snake. He won't be collecting any bounties on the Trains or anyone else for some time to come."

"I'm relieved to hear that," Marion returned.

"Did he mention anything about his encounter with Matt Train?" Della ventured.

Harrigan read the concern on Della's face. "You know about the Train family, do you?"

Della felt that she should not have spoken out but she had to know the answer to her question. "Oh . . . Aunt Marion has been telling me all about them."

"That's right," Marion interceded. "We've been discussing their troubles."

"Troubles, no doubt, created by Clegg Ralston," Harrigan replied.

"Yes, Aunt Marion told me about him as well."

Marion nodded at Harrigan.

"I see," he said. "Well, Snake didn't have much to say. The story he's telling is that Matt Train sneaked up on him from behind. Anybody familiar with Snake Danford knows that that's a fabrication, and anybody who knows Matt Train knows that Matt's too good with a gun to have to do anything like that."

Della listened closely.

"Matt patched up Snake and sent him on his way. He did a pretty credible job too."

There was obvious relief on Della's face.

Harrigan glanced at Marion, who smiled.

"I'm afraid that Della is becoming personally involved in this Train matter, Doc. More than likely, I've influenced her rather heavily."

"Well, that's understandable."

"You recall I mentioned that Della's father was a newspaperman. Della seems to have inherited his curiosity. She can also be a bit of a crusader at times."

Della forced a laugh. "Maybe I do get overly involved in issues sometimes, but I've heard all about the Train family, and it seems obvious to me that they've been railroaded."

"Most folks around here will agree with you there," Harrigan returned.

"Amen," Marion added.

"Well, I have to get to the livery to pick up my buggy. I'll be talking to both of you very soon. Oh, by the way, Snake's had one visitor since he's been in town—Clegg Ralston."

"Somehow, that doesn't surprise me," Marion said. "He'll probably urge Snake to file additional charges against Matt Train."

Harrigan chuckled.

After the doctor left, Marion turned to Della.

"I know," Della said, feeling a bit foolish, "I shouldn't have said anything, but I was afraid for Matt when I heard the name Snake Danford."

"How did you know about Danford?"

"When Matt and I were riding to Slim's, Matt thought he saw Danford riding past us into the mountains. It was Matt who told me about him."

"I see."

"I'm afraid I'd never be much of an actress, Aunt Marion. I let my emotions get the best of me. Do you think that Doc Harrigan saw through me?"

"Probably. Doc doesn't miss much but I wouldn't worry. He's as good a man as there is, and he would never do anything to endanger the Trains," Marion explained as she placed a consoling hand on Della's shoulder.

Chapter Six

Late Sunday afternoon, Marion rented a buckboard. She and Della baked two apple pies and packed them into a picnic basket. They then started for Slim Holly's place.

They were barely halfway there when Marion nudged Della. "Don't look now but I think we're being followed."

"Who is it?"

"I can't tell for sure, but it's a man on horseback. I thought I saw him about five minutes ago, riding among those rocks along that ridge."

Della waited for a minute and then cast a furtive glance over her shoulder. She spotted a lone horseman at a distance of some two hundred yards.

"Who do you think it is, Aunt Marion?"

"I don't know."

"Maybe he isn't following us."

"Don't bet on it. It's a lonely stretch to Slim Holly's. Most likely, anybody riding in this direction from Questor is heading to Slim's."

Della felt uneasy as she shifted in her seat on the buckboard. "Do you think we should continue?"

"I don't think there would be any point in returning to town. Whoever's following us has a pretty good idea where we're going by now."

Della nodded.

"I'll bet it's Cord Renfro."

"Cord Renfro? Why would he be following us?"

"Don't you remember the way he looked at you back at the shop?"

Della shivered.

Marion reached for her handbag in the back of the buckboard and placed it between them.

Della glanced at her aunt.

"I have a gun if we need it." She shook the reins, and the horse moved at a quicker pace.

Twenty minutes later Slim Holly's ranch house came into sight. His hound began to bark, and they soon saw it leaping about near the barn.

Della recognized Slim's rail-like form as he stepped onto his porch. He eyed the approaching buckboard for some time and then waved off the dog. The hound lowered his head to the ground, tucked his tail between his legs, and slunk off.

"Why, good day, ladies," Slim said with a generous grin. "I didn't expect to see you so soon." He helped Marion and Della off the buckboard.

Marion carried her handbag, and Della picked up the picnic basket.

"Is that apple pie?" Slim asked, sniffing the air.

"It is," Marion replied. "We thought that you might enjoy some dessert."

"Why, come in, please."

Della followed Slim and her aunt up the steps. She paused on the porch and glanced at the road behind. She scanned the landscape in every direction but detected nothing. Still uncomfortable, she turned and entered the house.

Slim's place was much more livable than Della had imagined. For a bachelor, living alone, he kept a clean and tidy household. His furniture was nothing fashionable or fancy, but it appeared to be serviceable and comfortable. The kitchen was just off the parlor, where a round table covered with a white cloth sat in the middle of the room. Della handed the picnic basket to Slim, who placed it on the table. He removed the pies and grinned broadly as he set them on a counter.

"I sure do appreciate this, Miss Marion. You know what a sweet tooth I've got."

"I hope you enjoy them, Slim."

"I guarantee I will. Why, I'll polish off one of these tonight."

"But that's not the only reason we dropped by."

Slim's expression grew serious. "It's about the Trains, isn't it?"

Marion nodded. She turned to Della, who reached into her bodice and extracted the documents that she had discovered. She placed them in Slim's hands. "We have to get this information to Matt Train."

Slim glanced at the papers and then at Marion and Della.

Marion quickly summarized the contents.

Slim let out a low whistle. "I'm sure Matt will be coming by soon. I'll be glad to hold them for him." He cast a look around and then made his way to one of the shelves. He removed a tin canister labeled FLOUR and brought it back to the table. "I'll just slip the papers into the sugar," he announced.

"But, Slim, that isn't sugar. That tin says flour," Marion pointed out.

Slim grinned sheepishly. "Why, Miss Marion, you know I never learned to read."

Marion returned a sympathetic glance and watched as he unscrewed the lid to reveal a supply of sugar. He buried the papers beneath the granules and then secured the lid. "They'll be safe here with me."

"I'm certain they will, Slim," Marion replied. "There's one more thing. We were followed here from town . . . by Cord Renfro, I think."

"Renfro! That polecat! Why, I'll run him off my spread right now."

"No, Slim," Marion said, placing a restraining hand

on his arm. "I don't think he's anywhere nearby, but he knows we came out here. We don't want you to be in the middle of this, but you're the only one who has a chance of getting this information to Matt. He certainly can't come anywhere near town."

Slim grinned, and the skin on his face pulled tightly, revealing his high cheekbones and making his eyes look twice their size. "I dealt myself in this crazy poker game when I heard the Trains were in trouble, and I'll be here until the last card is played."

Marion smiled.

Della appreciated this man and respected his loyalty to the Trains. She felt that Slim would be the kind of friend she would want to have should she ever find herself in trouble.

"Are you ladies sure you don't want an escort back to town?"

"No, I don't think that will be necessary, Slim. You just stay here and make sure that Matt gets these papers . . . and let's hope it's soon," Marion said.

Matt Train left Bullwhip in the deep shadows of some boulders some hundred yards from his ranch house. A pass of his hand across the horse's muzzle told the animal that silence was of the essence. A quarter moon cast down scant light from a nearly cloudless sky. Except for the strident trill of a night bird, quiet blanketed that part of the valley occupied by the Train ranch house. Train had never looked at his home quite like this before—from this position and angle. His perspective gave him pause for thought, for despite its damaged state, it still appeared imposing as it stretched across the land like a sleeping giant waiting to be awakened by its missing inhabitants.

He had spotted the figures of two men near the wall at the front gate. They sat in the shadows, rifles cradled in their arms, watching for anyone who might chance to approach the estate. Train had seen them there before—usually two and sometimes three—as he chanced to return from time to time. The ranch house and out-buildings were too big, too sprawling, however, for a mere handful of men to cover them adequately. It would take at least a dozen, strategically positioned, to be able to prevent one from being able to enter. Even then, Train doubted that they could keep him out, for he knew every inch of the spread, having lived here his entire life.

He had a feel for the land. He knew distances, those objects that offered cover, the areas of concealment; he knew the ranch house as if it were a living thing—which floorboards creaked beneath the weight of his feet, which windows offered the least resistance, which rooms could be illuminated without being seen by those who might be watching. He was actually a bit puzzled by the halfhearted effort Ralston was making in posting only a few men at the ranch house. Perhaps it was because Ralston found it inconceivable that the Trains would even attempt to return, considering the risk. He may have simply concluded that they were miles away, with no intention of going anywhere near Questor. The guards might simply be there in the one-in-a-hundred chance that a member of the family would dare to show his face. Train was also curious as to why Ralston's men had never seemed to enter the ranch house. Perhaps such an action would prove too overt—even for the likes of Ralston. After all, the house, the buildings, and the land on which they stood were still Train property—for a while, at least.

Train surveyed the landscape between the ranch house and his position and then moved ahead, soundlessly, low to the ground. When he reached one of the rear windows, he paused, glanced to his left and right, and then raised the sash. He completed the action slowly, thereby minimizing the sound of wood sliding against wood, and pulled himself through the opening. When his boots touched the floor inside, he paused again and peered out the window. For a full minute he remained motionless, his back pressed against the wall as he watched and listened. Detecting nothing, he moved ahead cautiously, so as not to topple a piece of furniture.

A few feet down a hallway took him to the kitchen. He eased inside and reached into his pocket for a match. He struck the sulphur tip, casting a harsh glare about the room. In seconds, the glare mellowed and he selected one of a pair of candles from a shelf. This he lit and placed on a small table off in a corner. Quickly, he chose a large sack from a pile kept near a wood bin and began to stock it with airtights stored on some shelves. To this he added some sacks of sugar and coffee. When he was satisfied that he could carry no more, he left the sack on the floor and returned to the hallway. Utilizing the faint glow from the candle, which he left in the kitchen for fear its light would reveal his presence if he carried it to other rooms, he made his way down the hall until he reached a tall double door. Here, he paused again, listened for some time, and then pushed his way through the doors.

The room in which he found himself was in total darkness. He took a few steps to his right and then reached out until he felt a wooden frame. It was smooth to his touch, and he ran his hand across it until he encountered another piece of wood meeting the first at a right angle. Using his fingers, he felt a number of rectangular objects. He counted two from the left, slid the item out of its position, and then tucked it inside his shirt. This accomplished, he retraced his steps down the hallway to the kitchen. Here, he secured the sack, returned the candle to its original position, and blew it out. He waited a long moment for his eyes to acclimate to the darkness again and then made for the window.

Bullwhip was waiting for him among the boulders. The horse turned and acknowledged Train's presence with a slight toss of his head. Train tied the sack to his saddle horn, swung into the saddle, and urged the roan through the boulders.

It was late morning when Train rode up to the stone hut. He saw three horses secured to some scrub just off to the left of the structure. The door opened and his father emerged, a rifle held in his hand. Mort smiled when he recognized his son. He turned, called over his shoulder, and Sarah walked through the door, her face beaming at the sight of Matt.

Matt dismounted, threw his arm around his mother, and smiled at his father. He loosened the sack from the saddle horn and handed it to Mort. "Supplies from our own kitchen," he announced.

Sarah's expression suddenly turned serious. "Matt, I've told you before that I don't think it wise to go anywhere near the ranch house. Ralston is certain to have men posted there."

"He did but it was easy enough to avoid them. Besides, it would be an even greater risk to attempt to purchase supplies in a neighboring town."

"Slim could help," Mort suggested.

Sarah shook her head. "He's helped us so much already with clothes and such. I wouldn't want him to be placed in danger because of us."

"That's what true friends are for, Sarah," Mort returned. "We'd be there for him."

"That's true enough."

"Like it or not, I'm afraid we're going to have to rely on some of our good neighbors until this matter is cleared up. We really have no choice, Sarah."

She nodded, conceding the point reluctantly.

"Son, were you able to see Joe Winston in Grandville?" Mort asked.

Matt frowned. "I'm afraid not. I learned from a farmer just outside of Grandville that Joe has been suffering from rheumatism for years. He quit practicing law and moved back East to be with his daughter—over three years ago."

Mort shook his head in despair. "I've got a feeling that time's passed me by."

"There are other lawyers," Sarah interjected.

"Yeah, young ones who are short on principles and eager to make a dollar."

"Oh, Mortimer, don't be so depressing. There are plenty of fine young men out there who have respect for the law and for those in need of help," Sarah countered.

Mort grunted. "Any word on Frank Weldon?"

"I was planning on dropping in on Slim Holly tonight. He should be able to tell me if Marshal Weldon has arrived yet in Questor."

Mort passed his hand through his hair. "That's got me concerned too. He should've been here by now. The only way we're going to get out of this is with the law, and Weldon's the best. He's the only authority figure left I'd trust with my life."

"It could be, Pa, that Weldon never got Ben's telegram. He might be anywhere in the territory, occupied with another matter."

"That's possible, but if that's the case then we're in a deeper hole than I thought. Time's not on our side. It's on Ralston's. Something's got to break soon, or our situation is only going to get worse."

"I've got a feeling that things are going to turn for us soon. The Trains have swallowed enough dirt. It's time now that we turned the tables on Ralston."

Mort grinned. "You got something planned, boy?"

"Let's just say that it's time we made our own breaks."

Mort and Sarah exchanged glances, a new spirit radiating between them.

Sarah placed her hand on Matt's shoulder. "Son, you look a little worn. Have you had your lunch yet?"

Matt pushed back his Stetson. "I haven't had breakfast."

"Well, then you come right inside while I fix you something."

"You'll need to get some shuteye as well before you go traipsin' off again. How much sleep did you get last night?" Mort asked.

"Maybe four hours."

"Once you get some of your mother's cooking under your belt and some solid hours under a blanket, you'll feel fine again."

Matt washed and then made his way into the hut. His father was already seated at the table, and Matt sat down opposite him. He unbuttoned his shirt and removed the article that he had carried through the night. "By the way, Mother, I was able to borrow this from the library last night. I thought you might like to read it again while you're passing time up here in the mountains. It might keep your mind off our problems."

Sarah put down her bowl and stepped over to the table. Her eyes grew wide as she looked at the book. "Oh, *David Copperfield* . . . my favorite novel! Thank you, son," she said as she hugged him and kissed him on the cheek.

Matt glanced across the table and saw Mort grinning at him.

Chapter Seven

Lute Kagen had been on foot for the last hour. His mare had come up lame, and she was hobbling on three legs as he led her down the road. He paused and took a long pull of water from his canteen, swished it around in his mouth, and then spat it out. A dim light caught his eye from ahead, maybe fifty feet off the main road, among a cluster of rocks and some thick brush. He made a minute adjustment to his holster and then moved forward.

Kagen was tall, just over six feet, and he carried his one hundred eighty pounds in well-presented proportion. His suit and Stetson were dark and of fine quality, although now they were dust-covered from the trail. The most notable physical feature about him was his eyes. Dark and penetrating, they were the eyes of a searcher. In fact, over the past seven years, Kagen had made his living collecting bounties on wanted men. He was good with his gun, and he was an excellent tracker, but he also possessed a singular quality common to many in his line of work—he was utterly ruthless. Neither laws nor property rights meant anything to him. He avoided contact with the law whenever possible, save to bring in his victims, which in most cases, were packed across their saddles. Lawmen shunned him; most men crossed to the far side of the bar when he ordered a drink. It was a solitary life, but one that suited him completely, for he was a loner by nature, a man who cared little for the company of others.

Kagen approached the fire cautiously. He was cautious about most things he did. He spotted one man sitting on a rock, feeding sticks into the flames of a campfire. A sorrel was staked out some twenty feet away. Satisfied that the man was alone, Kagen advanced. He was within a few feet of the fire when the man turned suddenly and stared up at Kagen, his mouth agape.

"Mister, you sure scared the daylights out of me! You shouldn't come into a man's camp like that."

"You should be more alert. I understand that there are Apaches about," Kagen returned.

"Shucks, I wouldn't hear an Apache one way or the other but you sure move like one."

The man was young, in his early twenties, a cowhand by appearance.

"Your coffee smells good."

"Well, it sure enough is, and you're welcome to some.

Sorry I don't have any beans left, but I've got a couple of biscuits."

"The coffee will do me just fine."

Kagen watched as the cowhand lifted the coffeepot and filled a cup. He handed it to Kagen with a smile.

"It's good to have a body to talk to. I haven't seen a soul since noon yesterday."

"Where are you headed?"

"No place in particular. I'm just driftin' north lookin' for ranch work. Name's Jim Small."

Kagen took a sip of coffee as he eyed Small's horse.

Small turned as Kagen's mare whinnied. "Looks like your mount's come up lame. What happened?"

"She stepped into a prairie dog hole a ways back."

"I'll be glad to take a look at her. I'm a pretty fair hand when it comes to horses."

"Help yourself."

Small stepped over to the mare and patted her on the flank. As he ran his fingers up and down her foreleg, the mare tossed her head uneasily. "I don't think anything's broken, only a bad sprain. She just needs to rest is all."

"Unfortunately, I have an appointment, and I don't have time to rest her."

"Well, you sure as dirt can't ride her the way she is."

"I don't suppose you'd be interested in making a trade?"

Small eyed him warily. "Afraid not. I don't hanker

bein' stranded out here with a lame horse, but I'll be glad to ride double with you 'til we reach the next town."

Kagen shook his head as he stood and faced Small, his hand drifting toward his gun. "I don't think so. We're going in opposite directions, and like I said . . . I have an appointment."

Small's face seemed to freeze as he studied Kagen from across the fire. "You aren't serious?"

"I'm afraid I am."

"Why, you can't just stroll into a man's camp and then up and take his horse away like that."

Kagen did not reply.

Small's hand moved closer to his gun.

"Don't do it. You aren't fast enough," Kagen said flatly.

"I wouldn't be much of a man if I didn't fight for what's mine, would I?"

They faced each other for some twenty seconds from across the fire. Then, Small made his play. Kagen's hand moved fast. His gun was in his palm in an instant, and the hammer was cocked. Small's gun was still in its holster.

Kagen considered the cowhand for a long moment. Fear was written all over the young man's face. Finally, Kagen ordered, "Loosen your gun belt and toss it over here."

Small did as he was told.

"Now, trade my saddle and gear with yours."

"Oh, so you're at least goin' to leave me my saddle."

"Don't get smart, boy. I'm in a charitable mood.

Besides, I never waste a bullet on a man who isn't wanted by the law."

It was late when Matt Train rode onto Slim Holly's spread. He could see lights in the windows of the ranch house. The buildings were one shade darker than the night sky, providing him with a general conception of the layout. He detected no sounds and no activity, yet he remained in the saddle next to a massive boulder for some time, careful not to be outlined against the pale light of a crescent moon. Suddenly, he heard Slim's hound baying somewhere off in the distance, and then, about a hundred feet ahead, he thought he saw the dog leaping off in pursuit of some creature—probably a fox or coyote after some of Slim's chickens.

Train waited a bit longer and then urged the roan on, ever alert to anyone who might be lying in wait in the shadows. He dismounted, not in front of the house, but near the barn instead, where he secured the reins of his horse to a hitching rail and edged his way along the side of the barn. Here, he waited for several more minutes, eyeing the ranch house up close and from a different perspective than the one he had enjoyed from his position near the boulder. Content that all was normal, he made his way toward the house, slipping noiselessly up the steps and onto the porch. He moved to one of the windows and peered inside. The curtains were only partly drawn, and he could see Slim inside, sitting in his chair, mending a harness. He stepped to the door and tapped softly.

A moment later he heard Slim's feet shuffling across the floor.

"Who's there?"

"It's Matt," he said, barely above a whisper.

Quickly, the door opened, and Train slipped inside, closing the door after him. "Is everything quiet?" he asked.

Slim nodded. "It's good to see you, boy."

They shook hands.

"How are your ma and pa holdin' up?"

"As well as can be expected."

"That's good to hear. You look a little worn down."

"I've spent a lot of hours in the saddle lately."

"I've got some coffee on the stove, and there's apple pie in the cupboard."

"Sounds good," Train said, removing his Stetson and hanging it on a wall peg.

"Set yourself down while I get some plates."

Train pulled out a chair and sat down at the table. "Any word on Frank Weldon?"

"No. I checked when I drove Miss Della into town. He hasn't come to Questor yet."

Train frowned.

"But something just as important came up."

Train turned toward Slim anxiously.

Slim removed the canister from the shelf and placed it before Train, who regarded him curiously. "Open it. There's papers inside that came from Ben Connover."

"Ben?"

"That's right. Della found them in her handbag. She figured Ben must've slipped them into her bag after she was knocked out. He must've known that he'd be searched, so he took a chance that somehow the papers would find a way into your hands, and they sure enough did."

Train twisted the lid and removed the documents. He spread them out on the table before him and devoured them excitedly while Slim set the table and poured the coffee. When he finished reading, he did not speak. Instead, he ate some pie and drained his cup. Then, he reread everything carefully.

Slim said nothing. He knew that Train was too absorbed to be distracted, and he merely sat across the table from him and nursed his coffee.

Finally, Train pushed his plate away and eyed Slim. "This business about Ralston being wanted for questioning in Denver is something I never imagined. Connover did an excellent job of digging to discover this . . . but this is something for the law to handle. Webb Crane, on the other hand, is another matter. According to Ben's investigation, Crane is holed up in Clayton. I have to find him and bring him back. Before I'm through with him, he'll be begging to tell the truth about what really happened."

Slim nodded. "Crane is one hombre who bends with the wind. He's got about as much backbone as a bowl of mashed spuds."

"He's the only one who can clear my pa and me in the shootings of Sheriff Marbury and Rad Barlow. Ralston's boys won't talk, no matter what. If they do, their own necks will end up in a noose."

"You're going to Clayton, then?"

"Yes."

"That's near eighty miles—round trip."

"I'll make it. I have to."

"You're tired, boy. Not the kind of tired from a day of hard work, but the kind of tired that a man gets from bein' on the run."

Train shrugged. "I have to get this information to my folks before I go. If anything should happen to me, at least they'll have something to work on."

"Why don't you let me do that?"

Train regarded him closely.

"You've got enough of a ride ahead of you. I can save you some time by getting those papers to your folks."

"It can be dangerous if you're even seen anywhere near them."

Slim grinned. "Tell me about it."

Train grinned back. Finally, he nodded. "You know that old hut my pa built . . . up past the arch rocks?"

"Know it? Maybe your pa forgot to mention it, but I had a hand in constructing that dwelling. I even tried a little prospectin' with him before I tired of it and turned my attention to other matters—like horses."

"Well, they've been staying there for the last week or so."

Slim contemplated the situation. "Let's see, that'll take me close to a full day there and back."

"That's about right. Make sure you're not seen."

"Don't worry. I'll leave well before sunup. I'll be in the mountains before anybody with a notion for curiosity even knows I'm gone. Oh, and speakin' of curious, Miss Marion mentioned that she and Della were followed out this way when they brought the papers. She said she thought it was Cord Renfro."

"Renfro? He's a bad one."

"That he is."

"I can't imagine that Ralston could be on to my meeting up with Della."

"I can't see how either."

"Then again, Della was the only one who survived that attack on the stage. Ralston might just be having her watched in the hope that she might lead him to something useful."

"It's possible."

"Be more careful than ever. Double back on your trail from time to time, just in case."

"When I don't want to be found, even Sticks, my hound, can't track me."

Train smiled. "By the way, that's the best pie you ever made."

"I didn't make it. Miss Marion did."

"That figures."

It was early afternoon when Lute Kagen rode into Questor. He immediately noticed the name Ralston on a large sign. It stood out among all the other signs. He sat in the saddle for a long time, considering the layout of the main street, before he headed for the hotel.

An hour later, he had bathed, shaved, and changed into his only other suit. He made his way through the hotel lobby and crossed the street toward Ralston's place of business. Cord Renfro was sitting in the outer office, his Stetson pulled down low over his forehead, his chair tilted against the wall. He eyed Kagen curiously and then climbed to his feet. "You must be Lute Kagen," he said, a timorous tone in his voice.

Kagen did not respond. He merely stared at Renfro with his cold, penetrating eyes.

"Uh . . . Mr. Ralston is in his office. I'll tell him you're here."

Renfro disappeared through a door and returned within seconds. "Come in, Mr. Kagen. Mr. Ralston has been expecting you."

Kagen passed through the door. Ralston was behind his desk. He extended his hand, and Kagen took it. Both men assessed each other closely before sitting down.

Finally, Ralston reached into his desk and removed a packet of bills. "Two thousand dollars up front, as promised."

Kagen accepted the cash, thumbed through the stack of bills, and then placed them in the breast pocket of his coat.

Renfro stood behind Ralston, leaning against the wall near one of the windows. His eyes widened at the sight of the money.

"There's ten thousand more when the job is done," Ralston added.

"Suppose you fill me in on the details."

Ralston lit a cheroot, blew smoke into the air, and leaned back in his chair. For the next fifteen minutes, he provided Kagen with the essentials on the Trains, the deadline for the property taxes, and his attack on the stage.

Kagen listened intently. When Ralston concluded his remarks, he said, "Your assault on the stage was a mistake. You learned nothing from it. If the Trains' attorney obtained any information, you failed to discover what it was."

"I've come to realize that."

"Tell me about this woman who was left on the stage."

"Her name is Della Dorn. She's the niece of the town milliner. She's here for a visit. She just happened to be on the same stage as Connover."

"You're certain she can't connect your men to the attack?"

"Renfro here assures me that she can't. He's been keeping an eye on her ever since she got into town."

"Why?"

"Why . . . to be sure," Renfro put in.

"Then, you have doubts."

Renfro shuffled his feet uneasily. "I'm certain she couldn't have seen me, but . . . I just have a feeling about her."

"Has she done anything since you've been watching her to arouse any suspicions?"

"No. She's spent most of her time with her aunt in the milliner's shop. The only other thing she's done is ride out to Slim Holly's place."

"Slim Holly?"

"He's the man who found her at the stage wreck. He brought her into town," Ralston explained.

"Why would she go to Holly's place?"

Renfro shrugged. "My guess is to show her thanks for helping her. She and her aunt were toting a picnic basket."

"There doesn't seem to be anything in that," Kagen said.

"It is strange though that Holly would be anywhere near where the stage went down. His place is a long way from there," Ralston mused.

"Is there any connection between this Slim Holly and the Trains?"

Ralston nodded. "He's one of their best friends."

Kagen's eyebrow raised suddenly.

"Do you think there may be a connection somehow?"

Kagen considered the possibilities. "The woman was on the same stage as the Trains' attorney. Slim Holly, the Trains' close friend, just happened to be in the vicinity. You found nothing on the body of the attorney."

"Are you saying that the woman may be in possession of whatever it was that Connover may have discovered?" Ralston asked.

"It's possible. She was there."

Ralston ran his hand across his chin in thought.

"Did you search her?" Kagen asked, directing his question to Renfro.

"Why, no, of course not. Why would that lawyer entrust her with any important information? He didn't even know her."

Kagen shrugged. "I don't know, but it's worth looking into, especially since we don't have any other cards to play."

"I do have a man working on her now—my attorney," Ralston said. "He's seeing her socially. He's smart, cunning."

Kagen nodded. "All right, there's more than one way to skin a cat. We'll give him his chance but if he fails to get anywhere with her . . ."

Ralston and Renfro exchanged glances.

Kagen regarded Ralston narrowly. "I've got a pretty good notion of just how deep you are in this game, but before I start to operate I want to hear it from you."

Ralston returned his stare. "I don't want to have to look over my shoulder the rest of my life."

"As long as we understand each other."

Ralston placed his cheroot in an ashtray. "Where will you begin?"

Kagen considered the question. "From what you've told me, the Trains know this land better than anyone. If your men haven't been able to run them to ground after all this time, the chances are I won't do any better."

Ralston and Renfro focused on Kagen.

"When you want to kill a coyote, you don't track it into the brush. You arrange for it to come to you," Kagen stated.

"And just how do you do that?" Renfro asked.

"You build a chicken coop."

Both men regarded Kagen quizzically.

"If this Della Dorn happens to know anything at all about this matter, we may be able to use her to smoke out the Trains."

Ralston inhaled deeply on his cheroot. He held the smoke in his lungs for a long time before releasing it. A trace of a smile formed on his lips.

Renfro turned suddenly toward the window. "There she is now, along with her aunt."

Kagen and Ralston got to their feet and went to the window. For some time, they watched as Della and Marion made their way down the boardwalk and disappeared around the corner.

Kagen smirked. "Well, gentlemen, this may be even more interesting than I thought. I do believe we may have our chickens—and such pretty feathers."

As promised, Charles Ames sent a youngster by the millinery with a note for Della, asking if he could call on her for dinner at seven o'clock that evening. Della scribbled a reply of "yes." She was genuinely excited about the concept of seeing the dashing young attorney again, even if she was a bit wary of his intentions. She found herself a little distracted as she waited on customers for the remainder of the day.

That evening, she bathed, pinned up her hair, and put on the best dress she had packed for her visit to Questor. It was apple green with a lace collar and matching cuffs. Her Aunt Marion, who was more excited about the date than Della, loaned her her favorite cameo pin.

Ames called for her at precisely the designated time. He wore a black suit and derby hat. A gold watch fob dangled from his vest pocket, and Della thought that he looked every bit the distinguished professional that he was. He took her arm and assisted her into the buggy. They rode the short distance to the restaurant, where they were warmly greeted by the manager and led to a corner table that had been reserved for them. Ames pulled out the chair for Della and helped to seat her.

"I hope you'll like the dinner menu, Della. It isn't as sophisticated as something you might see in St. Louis or New York City, but the beef is tender, and the portions are generous."

"I've never been finicky, Charles, and I think this is a very nice place."

"That's what I like—a woman who is easy to please," he said with a grin.

Della smiled.

"How are things going in the millinery?"

"Oh, it's interesting. I've met some nice people. There's one lady who drops in every day for a chat."

"Ah, that would be the good Mrs. Ginger."

"Why, yes. How did you know?"

"Everyone in town knows Mrs. Ginger. She's a fount of information."

They both chuckled.

The waiter arrived with menus and shortly thereafter took their orders. Ames requested wine. A bottle and two goblets soon arrived, and Della and Ames sampled it. Della thought it was extremely good, and it put her in a comfortable mood. Their conversation was light and pleasant, and they were never at a loss for words. The dinner was tasty and filling, and Della found herself enjoying Ames' company very much.

A dessert of apple pie and coffee was served, and Della and Ames expanded their topics of conversation to include the law, Abraham Lincoln, the cattle business, and the latest in hats. Finally, Ames steered the discussion in the direction he had originally intended.

"Della, have you given any thought to what I said earlier about the newspaper business?"

"A little."

"Do you think that a St. Louis woman like you could handle small-town life?"

"Oh, it isn't that. What I've seen of Questor I like. I wouldn't have any problems living here."

Reaching into his pocket, Ames removed a folded newspaper. "I thought you might enjoy looking at a copy of our weekly. It just came out this afternoon." He opened it and passed it across the table to Della.

Della accepted it and scanned the first page. Her eyes

widened when she saw that the lead article concerned the Train family. Eagerly, she began to read the column. It provided some basic background information on the Trains, indicated that they were still at large, and detailed the charges and evidence against them. The reporter then went on to recount an interview he had conducted with Snake Danford, in which the bounty hunter claimed that he was ambushed by Matt Train, thereby giving rise to speculation that the Trains were still in the area. Della had not realized that for nearly five minutes she had been absorbed in reading the article when Ames suddenly took her off guard with a comment.

"It looks like Matt Train is getting desperate—shooting a man from ambush."

Without looking up from the paper, Della replied, "Matt would never do—" She looked up to find Ames' eyes intent upon her. She knew that she had allowed herself to become entrapped. "Matt Train would never do anything like that," she said, completing her remark.

"You talk as though you know him personally."

"No, of course, I don't. I've never met him. It's just that everything I've heard about him and his family has been of a positive nature. My aunt speaks very highly of all of them."

"Ah, that's merely the loyalty of a friend talking. As an attorney, I have the job of separating fact from feelings. That's the only way one can arrive at the truth."

Della breathed an inward sigh of relief. At their first meeting, she had sensed that, for some reason, Ames had doubted her version of the stage attack. Now, she was even more convinced of it. She thought that she had successfully managed to divert his suspicions or, at least, created some question in his mind with the way she responded following her slip of the tongue. Suddenly, she felt uneasy. They continued to discuss the Train family for a few minutes, but she was guarded in her comments, alert now to any attempt Ames might make to learn something from her.

Following the meal, Della and Ames made their way back to the buggy and then returned to Marion's house. As Ames walked Della to the door, he took her arm and turned her toward him.

"I've enjoyed your company, Della. I hope our differences over the Train family don't come between us."

"I hope not either."

"It's just that, as an attorney, I tend to approach matters from a cold, analytical point of view."

"But all the evidence isn't in."

"True, but based upon everything that I've seen and heard, it isn't hard to form an opinion."

"You know, from time to time, my father wrote about trials in his newspaper. There was a little rhyme that he used to publish when he thought that an injustice was being done or things were moving a little too fast. I can't remember the author, but it went something like this . . . *'The hungry judges soon the sentence sign, And wretches hang that jurymen may dine.'* "

Ames regarded her closely.

"Thank you for dinner, Charles."

"I hope that I can see you again."

"I hope so too."

He placed his hand under her chin and raised it gently. He looked into her eyes for a long moment and then kissed her tenderly. "Good night, Della."

"Good night," she replied, smiling back at him.

Ames touched the brim of his hat and left.

For a long time, Della stood in the darkness before opening the door. She was confused in her feelings toward Ames. He was an intelligent, sophisticated man who treated her with respect, yet she was uncertain as to his convictions and still pondered the real reason why he wanted to see her. Was he truly interested in her as a woman, or did he have some ulterior motive for asking to see her? Was he simply trying to ply information from her—information that could be used to locate and apprehend the Trains? She did not know the answers, and she went to bed that evening filled with doubts.

Ames recognized that Della knew more about the Trains than she was willing to reveal. Whatever the reason was he did not know. Perhaps it was sympathy; perhaps it was something more personal. What he did know was that she was a woman to whom he was attracted, a woman he thought he could love and be with. At first, seeing her was just a means to an end, but now he realized that there could be something more between them. She could prove to be an asset to his life and in his career if he were able to win her over; yet it was obvious that she was also a woman of principle. Once the Trains had ultimately been found and disposed of, how would she react to him? He was troubled over the matter as he drove the buggy back to the livery.

He made the walk to Ralston's office, a walk that he suddenly found he did not want to make. Ralston was standing near the window, staring out into the night when Ames entered. There was a kerosene lamp on the desk, casting a soft circle of light over the middle of the room, leaving the corners in shadows. Another man was present, sitting in a chair off to the side, his leg dangling casually over the armrest. Ames could not see his face.

"Did you learn anything new from the woman?" Ralston asked.

"No. She doesn't know anything," Ames answered.

"Well, Kagen here thinks there just might be a link somewhere."

Ames looked at the man in the shadows.

"Oh, Lute Kagen . . . Charles Ames," Ralston said by way of an introduction.

Ames recognized the name at once. It sent chills up his spine. He stared hard at the gunfighter but was still unable to penetrate the darkness that shielded his face. "And on what does he base such an opinion?"

"That's nice legal talk," Kagen said.

"It serves its purpose," Ames returned sharply.

Kagen slowly stood up and stepped to the middle of the room where he stood face to face with Ames. "I've got no evidence as you put it, counselor. I only have a hunch based on a series of facts. Maybe I'm right . . . maybe I'm wrong. Either way, if we can force the issue . . . we'll know for sure one way or the other."

"There's no point in hurting a young woman who knows nothing about any of this."

"If she knows nothing, all we've wasted is time. On the other hand, if she does know more than she's letting on . . . well, then that's another matter."

"It's a wild goose chase," Ames persisted.

"There's too much at stake not to take even the slimmest chance," Ralston interceded, regarding Ames closely.

"And if you're wrong, what happens to the woman?"

"That won't be your concern, Ames," Ralston said, turning away from him and staring out the window again.

Chapter Eight

Train saw the buzzards circling not far ahead. He reined in the roan and pulled his Winchester from its scabbard. Searching for some high ground, he spotted a rocky knoll not far off and turned Bullwhip in that direction. He dismounted and tied the horse to some scrub. The ascent was gradual, but the change in elevation was enough to give him a clear view of the surrounding area for some three hundred yards. Not far below, he saw the body of a man, an arrow protruding from his side. Some twenty feet beyond lay a horse, motionless, its head turned toward the ground, a small stream of blood covering its flank.

For several minutes, Train remained on the high ground, scanning the terrain in every direction. Experience had taught him that one could never be completely certain about Apaches, but when he was reasonably confident that there was no one else in the area, he descended the knoll, climbed onto Bullwhip, and made his way to the man.

Approaching cautiously, he dismounted a few feet from the man and turned him over on his back. A low moan told him the man was still alive. The arrow was buried deep in his side and had done some serious damage. Train knew at once that it was only a matter of time. The man looked to be about sixty-five. His skin was wrinkled from long exposure to the sun. His face was covered with a gray beard. He was small in build—not more than one hundred and thirty pounds. His clothes were, at one time, of good quality, although they were now old and worn. His boots were badly scarred, and the heels were worn. Train examined the man's hands. They were heavily calloused, with stubs for fingernails.

The man moaned again. Train quickly retrieved his canteen and his blanket roll. He placed the blanket under the man's head, moving him as gently as possible. As he did so, the man opened his eyes and focused on Train.

"Don't . . . don't move me."

Train poured some water over the man's lips. At first, it spattered onto his face; then, the man took several swallows.

Train studied the arrow shaft. He wrapped his fingers around it tightly as he contemplated extracting it.

"No . . . I tried that. Don't touch it. It'll only kill me that much sooner," the man uttered in a feeble voice.

Train nodded. He knew the man was right. There was nothing he could do but make the man as comfortable as possible.

"Name's Shamrock . . . Ed Shamrock."

"Matt Train."

"Good to know you, Matt."

"I'll try to get you to a doctor."

Shamrock smiled. "Now, you know that would be a waste of time. I'm not long for this world."

"What happened here?"

"A couple of Apaches jumped me. I winged one of 'em but by then it was too late."

"You're a prospector?"

Shamrock nodded. "I've got the look, I suppose."

Train smiled.

"Mr. Train, would you be an honest man?"

Train thought it a strange question. He wondered if the man were delirious. "Yes," he answered.

"I guess it wouldn't make much difference one way or the other if you weren't, seein' as how I don't have much choice," he said, managing a laugh.

Train offered him some more water but he waved it away.

"I've got to ask a favor of you, Mr. Train. You've got to promise me you'll do it, since there's no one else I can ask."

Train listened.

Shamrock pointed feebly in the direction of the dead horse. "In my saddlebag . . . there's a pouch of dust. It's not much to show for all the years I've spent in these mountains—only four or five hundred dollars . . . but it's enough to do what needs to get done."

"Go on."

"I want you to take it and deliver it to a woman. She lives on a spread some ten miles northeast of here. I was on my way there when I had this . . . accident."

"Mr. Shamrock, I—"

"Now, don't tell me about your problems. I've got my own as you can see."

Train remained silent.

"This woman has got some problems of her own. I was hopin' to help her but I can't. That means that some-body else has to. There must be a reason why the Good Lord sent you by here, and I reckon it was to finish off the job that I couldn't do."

"Who is this woman?"

"Her name's Carver . . . Erin Carver. She's my daughter. She's got a five-year-old boy . . . Eddie, named after me." Shamrock's eyes seemed to shine at the thought of the boy. "She's caught up in a bad marriage. She wants to get out but she can't. That gold dust will stake her to some stage tickets and a new start."

Train was reluctant to agree to honoring Sham-rock's request, but he did not see how he could refuse a dying man. "All right, Mr. Shamrock, I'll deliver your dust."

Shamrock smiled. "God bless you for it, Mr. Train."

Train meted out a bit more water to him, and Shamrock swallowed it with difficulty.

"Is there anything you want me to say to your daughter?"

Shamrock shook his head. "There's nothing that can be said. I've let her down—too many times. I've been a big disappointment to her. I was a failure all my life at everything I did—farming, ranching, business, even prospecting."

"Looks like you had some luck."

Shamrock forced a smile, though it was obvious that it pained him. "Scratchings is all. It took too long, and maybe it's even too late."

"I can't believe that."

"Thanks for bein' hopeful, but the truth of the matter is that there's not much left between Erin and me."

"I'll make sure that your daughter gets the gold."

Shamrock nodded. "By the way, are you any good with that .45?"

"Yes."

"You may have to use it. Erin's husband, Rafe Carver, is a dangerous man. He'll do anything to keep her."

"Like I said, I'll make sure that your daughter gets the gold."

Shamrock smiled. He spoke little after that, and in an hour he stopped breathing.

Train buried him where he died. He piled rocks on top of his grave and then fashioned a cross out of some branches. He located the pouch of dust in one of the saddlebags as Shamrock had indicated and mounted up.

As he rode, Train wrestled uncomfortably with his thoughts. His journey was interrupted by an errand for a man who died a lonely death and a woman he did not know. He had his own problems, and every hour that he delayed in reaching the town of Clayton could increase his chances of losing Webb Crane. Yet a ride to the Carver spread was not that far out of his way. Perhaps he could honor Shamrock's request and still locate Crane without sacrificing anything more than time.

He followed the old man's directions until he came upon a rundown spread just off the road to Clayton. Both the house and barn were badly in need of repair. A few chickens scratched about in the dirt, and a scrawny looking milk cow stood near a pasture gate. Train took in the scene for some time before riding up to the house and dismounting. He dropped Bullwhip's reins over a hitching rail and walked up to the porch. A woman opened the door and stepped out. She was young and pretty, with delicate features and light brown hair, but there was a strain on her face as though she were worn out. It was the kind of strain that suggested worry and fear. A small boy trailed behind her. His hair was red, and his eyes were large and inquisitive. He wore faded coveralls and his shoes were threadbare.

Train touched the brim of his Stetson. "I'm looking for Erin Carver."

"I'm Erin Carver." The woman eyed him curiously.

"I'm sorry to have to inform you that your father is dead."

The words did not seem to have any effect on her for some time. Then, she raised a trembling hand to her lips and closed her eyes tightly as if to wish away the words she had just heard.

The boy looked up at his mother and then stepped closer to her, placing his small arm around her waist. She glanced down at him and then moved him in front of her, resting her hands on his shoulders as he faced Train.

"How did it happen?" Erin asked.

"Apaches. I found him about ten miles to the south. He was on his way here when he was ambushed."

Erin's lips tightened. "I haven't seen my father for a long time. He was always good to me . . . and to Eddie here. I . . . I don't really know what to say."

"There's never much anyone can say about death. I suppose all we can do is hold on to memories for as long as we can."

Erin nodded. "I . . . I'd invite you in, Mr . . ."

"Just call me Matt."

"I'd invite you in, Matt, but my husband may be back any time now, and he wouldn't like it. He's . . . he's not a very sociable man."

"I understand. I can't stay anyway. I have business in Clayton." Train shifted his weight awkwardly. "You'll forgive me for saying this, but your father spoke to me for some time before he passed on. He told me that you were . . . unhappy in your . . . situation."

Erin's lips pursed together as tears rolled down her cheeks.

Train pulled the sack of gold from his saddlebag and placed it on a bench at Erin's feet. "He was on his way to you with this when he was attacked. He said it would buy you a fresh start wherever you wanted to go."

Erin stared at the sack of gold as though dumbfounded.

"There's between four and five hundred dollars there. Your father worked hard for it. He said that it was all he could do to help."

Eddie looked up at his mother and smiled.

Erin wiped the tears from her cheeks with the back of her hand as she smiled back at her son. "My father was a good man, Matt. He always considered himself a failure but I never did."

"I don't know how he lived, Erin, but he died thinking of you and your boy."

"Thank you . . . for that."

"If there's nothing else I can do, I'd best be on the move," Train said as he stepped toward his horse.

"There's nothing else. Goodbye Matt."

Just as Train started to mount, he heard Erin cry out.

"Oh my God! It's Rafe! He's coming back from town," she uttered, panic written on her face.

Train turned and saw a rider approaching.

Erin began to whimper, and Eddie clutched the folds of her dress as he turned and buried his face against her. "Matt, you'd best leave now while you can. Rafe won't understand. You can ride off through the fields."

The last thing that Train wanted was trouble, but he had no intention of running at the sight of a man he did not know.

Carver rode in hard and fast. He dismounted some ten feet from Train and slapped sharply at his horse's flank. The animal lurched before trotting off toward the barn. Carver was a stout-looking man of about Train's size. He wore a battered Stetson, a plaid shirt, and wide suspenders that held up a pair of dirty pants. He had a crooked nose that set off a mouth that twisted severely to one side, making him look as if he were sneering. "Who are you, mister?" Carver asked, his cold eyes lancing through Train.

"He . . . he brought word of my father's death, Rafe," Erin said in a quavering voice.

"I asked him," Rafe snapped, pointing a beefy hand at Train.

"It's as she says, Mr. Carver."

Carver glanced at Erin. "As soon as I turn my back you're at it. I never could trust you."

"Rafe, please, it's not like that."

"Shut your mouth! I'll deal with you later. Right now, this saddle tramp is goin' to get what he's got comin' to him."

"Look, Mr. Carver, I—"

"The time for talkin' is over, mister. Right now, I aim to pound you into the ground and then grind you under my boot."

Carver was unarmed, and Train wondered exactly what the man had in mind as he rolled up his shirt sleeves and advanced toward Train.

"Please don't hurt him, Rafe. He didn't do anything. He only came here to help us," Erin pleaded from the porch.

"You're making a mistake, Carver."

"You're the one who made the mistake, saddle tramp!" Carver said through gritted teeth as he swung a round-house right at Train.

Train could smell liquor on Carver's breath as he sidestepped the swing, drew his Colt and brought it down against the side of Carver's head.

Carver stood in place, stunned for a long moment before he collapsed to his knees. His eyes rolled around in their sockets, and then he fell forward to the ground.

Train shook his head and then holstered his .45. "I'm sorry I had to do that," he said to Erin.

Erin pressed her hand to her lips and then patted Eddie reassuringly on his back. "You had no choice, Matt. Rafe goes crazy sometimes."

"I'm sure he'll be all right in a while. I tried not to hit him too hard."

"He's got a head like a rock, and not much passes through it."

"Do you want me to help you get him inside?"

"No, I hope to be gone by the time he comes to."

Train was a bit surprised by her remark.

"I'd appreciate it, Matt, if you would do me one more favor before you go. Would you catch up Rafe's horse and harness him to our buckboard?"

"All right."

"I'm going to pack some things for Eddie and me."

Train did as Erin asked. The horse had run into the barn, where Train found it in one of the stalls. He un-saddled it and led it over to a buckboard, which sat near the door. Train went to work and had the horse in place when he heard a scream. Bullwhip then began to neigh excitedly. Train exited the barn in time to see Carver circling Erin near the porch. Carver held a sickle in his hand as he advanced closer and closer toward her. Eddie was standing by the door, crying in fear. Train pulled his Colt and took aim, but he held his fire when Bullwhip reared and then ambled toward Carver. The horse brushed against Carver, knocking him to the ground, and then suddenly reared again, brandishing his hooves high in the air. Carver roared in terror as he attempted to shield himself with his arms, but it was little defense against the powerful blows that Bullwhip inflicted.

Erin gasped in horror as she buried her face in her hands.

Train ran to Bullwhip and took hold of the animal's reins, pulling him away from Rafe Carver's bloody re-mains. Bullwhip continued to snort and pace back and forth in agitation for some time, but Train patted him down and walked him away from the scene, tying him to a post near the barn. Train then retraced his steps to Erin, who was weeping uncontrollably. He wrapped his arm around her and walked her back to the porch. "Get a blanket . . . and look after the boy. He needs you now," Train directed.

Erin gathered herself, nodded, and went to Eddie, who was clutching the door and sobbing. She picked him up and carried him inside. A few minutes later she emerged, carrying a blanket. Train took it and draped it over Carver's remains.

"He was out of his head," Erin said, staring at the motionless form beneath the blanket. "He got like that sometimes . . . when things were bad."

"It's a hard thing for a boy to have to see this happen to his father."

"Rafe wasn't Eddie's father."

Train glanced at her.

"Eddie's father died in a river crossing when we came West. Eddie was only a year old. I met Rafe a little over a year ago. He was good and kind and was willing to look after us. We married a few months after we met. For a while, things were good between us. Then, the farm failed, and Rafe started to drink. He turned sour . . . mean. He questioned my fidelity, although I never gave him any reason to. As to the rest, well, it's a story I'm sure you've heard before."

Train nodded. "I'm sorry."

"Don't be. The truth of the matter is that if this hadn't happened, Rafe would've most likely hanged for killing somebody else . . . maybe even me. I'm ashamed to have to say it but I'm glad he's dead."

Her words were hard but Train understood her feelings. The brief glimpse he had had of Rafe Carver had not been a pretty one. He shuddered to think what damage such a man might have done to the frail woman or to her little son. "Is there anything I can do?"

"No. I have neighbors close by. They're good people, and they know what Rafe was like. In a while, after Eddie has calmed down, the two of us will ride over. We can stay with them. They'll help me bury Rafe."

"What will you do then?"

"I'll see about selling the farm. Then, Eddie and I will head east, I suppose. Wherever we go, I can't imagine that it will be any worse than the life we've had over the past year."

Train nodded.

"I'm only sorry that you had to get mixed up in this." She extended her hand, and Train took it.

"Good luck, Erin."

"And to you, Matt."

Della and Marion had dinner at the house of one of Marion's friends. They enjoyed a meal of pork chops, mashed potatoes and greens and then talked for an hour over pie and coffee. It was dark when they returned home. Marion unlocked the front door and dropped her handbag on a side table. Della followed her in and removed her hat.

"I think it was altogether a good day, Aunt Marion. I like your shop and your friends."

"Yes, Questor is a nice town. I've been happy here," Marion said as she disappeared into the kitchen.

"I wouldn't mind spending some more time here. That is, if you wouldn't mind putting up with me for a while longer." She hesitated as she waited for her aunt's reply but it did not come. "Aunt Marion?" Della heard nothing for a long moment, and she followed her aunt into the kitchen. The room was dark, and she could barely see the table in front of her. "Aunt Marion, why haven't you lit the lamp?" As she took a step forward, she felt someone grab her from behind, and then a hand clamped down over her mouth. She panicked and started to struggle, but the arms that held her were like steel, and she could not budge under the pressure; nor could she call out, for the fingers that gripped her mouth prevented her from doing so.

A moment later, she heard a scratching sound, and the harsh glare of a match blinded her. When her eyes adjusted, she saw a man standing before her, his left arm wrapped tightly around her aunt's mouth, his right hand holding a match to the oil lamp on the table.

"I believe that I have the pleasure of addressing Miss Marion Vale and her niece Della," the man announced with a malevolent grin. "The name is Kagen . . . Lute

Kagen, and I'm sure you've already made the acquaintance of my colleague."

Della did her best to turn her head. She became even more alarmed when she saw that it was Cord Renfro who was restraining her. She squirmed even harder to break his hold but she saw that it was of no use.

"Now, we're all going to sit down here at the table and have a nice friendly talk, and no one is going to scream." He pulled a knife from his coat sleeve and held it to Marion's throat. Marion's eyes grew wide with terror. "Do I make myself clear?"

Marion nodded and Della followed suit.

Slowly, Kagen released his hand from Marion's mouth. She remained silent, and he moved the knife away from her throat.

Renfro relaxed his grip on Della's mouth. She released her breath, not realizing that she had been holding it.

Kagen nodded to them. Marion sat down, and Della dropped into the chair opposite her. Kagen sat between them while Renfro remained standing behind Della.

"Now, all we want is a little information. As soon as we get it, we'll be glad to leave your home," Kagen explained.

"I don't know what you mean," Marion said.

Kagen smiled. "I think you do."

Marion and Della looked at each other closely.

"I understand, Miss Dorn, that you were on the same stage with Ben Connover."

Della nodded.

"I believe that he was in possession of certain . . . information . . . that was not on him at the time of the stage attack. Therefore, he must have passed on that information to you, since you were the only other passenger on the stage."

"I don't know what you're talking about. He never gave me anything. We barely even talked except to exchange pleasantries and to chat about the ride—that sort of thing."

Kagen regarded her narrowly. "Why did the two of you visit Slim Holly?"

"Why, to give him some pies as a way of thanking him for helping me after the stage attack."

"Not to give him anything . . . from Ben Connover?"

"No. I told you, I received nothing from Mr. Connover," Della insisted.

Kagen felt the blade of the knife with his finger. "What we have here is a strange series of coincidences." He took a splinter out of the table's surface with the tip of the knife. "First, the Trains' lawyer is on a stage, but he is traveling empty-handed . . . no papers, no documents on his person. Did you ever hear of a lawyer returning from a business trip without papers?" He removed a larger splinter a few inches from the first. "Second, you happened to be on the same stage." He dug out still a third splinter from the tabletop. "Next, you visited Slim Holly, who just happens to be one of the Trains' closest friends."

"As I explained to you, it's just that—a coincidence, nothing more."

"Except for one thing . . . I don't believe in coincidences!" he raged as he raised the knife over his head and slammed it into the table, burying the blade halfway to the hilt.

Della and Marion recoiled in fear.

"Why don't you let me take the young one into the back room? I'll get it out of her," Renfro said.

Della blanched at his remark.

"No, I've got a better idea. Why don't we take the ladies out to Slim Holly's place for a visit. I understand it's quiet out there and isolated. I've got a feeling that when everyone is together again—like one big happy family—we'll learn the truth, one way or the other. Besides, I always did like socials."

Renfro laughed.

Della looked to her aunt for some sign, but Marion only stared back blindly, as if she were in some deep trance.

Chapter Nine

It was dusk when Matt Train entered the town of Clayton. Lamps were lit in many of the buildings. Street traffic was at a minimum. He pulled the roan into an alley at the rear of the hotel and dismounted. He moved on foot past some crates and barrels until he reached the street, where he watched and waited. Train knew that there were dodgers on him throughout the territory. To assume that they had not yet reached Clayton would be running too great a risk. Besides, he was known here. He had been in Clayton on business just over a year ago. He had stayed in the hotel. Even if dodgers had not yet arrived for posting, word of the reward on his head might have spread to many within the community. It simply would not pay to show his face if he could avoid it.

150

When he deemed it reasonably safe to walk on the main street, he edged his way around the corner and stepped onto the boardwalk. He slipped up to the window at the front of the hotel and stood just off to its side, peering through the curtains into the lobby. There was the usual complement of chairs and settees. One man was sitting beside a lamp reading a newspaper. A desk clerk sat on a stool behind the counter. Train did not recognize him from his last visit.

According to Ben Connover's report, Webb Crane was using the name Hastings. Train's next move was to learn Crane's room number. Should he take the chance that he might not be recognized and simply walk in and confront the desk clerk? Considering the fact that he did not remember the clerk, the odds might be in his favor, but was the risk worth taking at all? As he contemplated the situation, he saw a young boy of about fourteen approaching. Suddenly, he had an idea. He called the youngster over and placed a coin in his hand. "Would you run an errand for me?" Train asked, holding his head down low so that his face was shielded from the boy.

The boy examined the coin and grinned broadly. "Sure, mister, what is it?"

Train removed a pencil stub and a scrap of paper from his shirt pocket. He folded it twice and quickly scribbled Mr. Hastings on it. "Hand this to the desk clerk inside."

"That's all?"

"That's all."

The boy shrugged. "Sure, mister, but you could save yourself some money by doin' it yourself. The clerk's sittin' right in there."

"Just do it, boy," Train said, placing his hand on the youngster's shoulder and urging him toward the door.

Train watched through the window as the youngster entered the lobby and passed the note to the desk clerk. The clerk read the name on the paper and then turned and placed it into a slot behind him. By the time the boy emerged from the lobby, Train was gone.

The wooden steps leading to the second floor of the hotel were rickety, creaking and even swaying under Train's weight. He climbed them cautiously, pausing twice to glance at the alley below to see if he were being observed. When he reached the second floor landing, he opened the door and stepped inside, finding himself alone in a long, dimly lit corridor. Two rooms down on his right was Room 203. A crack of light was visible just under the door. Train held his ear to the door and listened. After a full minute, he heard a noise from within as if someone were moving on some bedsprings. He wrapped his hand around the doorknob and turned it—locked. He tapped softly.

There was no response from inside.

Again, he knocked, this time louder.

"Who is it?" a shaky, nervous voice returned.

Train recognized the voice as Webb Crane's. "Train . . . Matt Train."

There was a sharp intake of breath followed by a long pause.

"Open the door, Webb. We have to talk."

"Go away, Matt. I can't help you, and I don't want to talk to you."

"I'm not leaving, Webb."

"If you don't, I'll send for the sheriff. You're a wanted man." Crane's tone was strident, desperate.

Train did not hesitate. He threw his shoulder against the door, breaking off the lock and splintering the woodwork. Crane was standing near the bed. He was wearing his shirt and pants, but his boots were off as if he were preparing for bed. He was obviously shocked at the sight of Train.

Train closed the door behind him and turned to face Crane.

"How . . . how did you find me?"

"That's not important."

"What . . . what do you want with me, Matt?"

"I've come to take you back, Webb. You're going to tell the truth about what happened. You're the only one left who can clear my father and me."

Crane ran his hand through his hair nervously. His mouth twitched and his eyes grew large. "You can't ask me to do that. They'll kill me—the way they killed Steve Payton."

"I'll see that you get protection."

"From Ralston and all his gunfighters? How can you protect me? You're on the run yourself."

"I'll take you to another jurisdiction."

Crane licked his lips in agitation. "No, it won't work. I won't do it. I'm not going."

Train stepped forward and grabbed Crane by his shirt, pulling him up against him so that their faces were only an inch apart. "You're going, Webb, if I have to hogtie you and throw you over the back of a horse, but you're going," Train said flatly.

"Look, Matt, I understand how you must feel, but there's nothing I can do."

"Ralston's men killed Sheriff Marbury, and I shot Rad Barlow to prevent him from lynching my father."

"I know that."

"Yet you and Steve Payton didn't tell it that way."

"We were afraid! Clegg Ralston threatened both of us. He said that if we didn't back his version of the story, he'd kill us. Payton decided to square things, and look what it got him."

"I heard about Payton. Everybody in Questor but the fools know that Ralston was responsible for his death, but without your testimony I'll never be able to clear myself."

"Not a chance, Matt. I'm dead if Ralston finds out that I changed my story."

"I don't think you understand, Webb. You're going back, and we're leaving now. Get your boots on," Train ordered as he shoved Crane backward onto the bed.

Crane eyed Train nervously, shaking his head in disbelief as he fumbled with his boots. "This isn't going to work, Matt. Half the people in the territory want to collect the bounty on your head, and Ralston will have me shot on sight if he even knows I'm with you."

"Suppose you let me worry about that," Train countered as he picked up Crane's coat and tossed it to him.

Crane stood up and slipped into his coat.

"Where do you stable your horse?"

"I sold my horse when I got to town. I was planning on lying low for a while and then taking a stage north."

"We'll have to buy one for you."

Train opened the door and checked the hallway. It was empty. Quietly, he led Crane to the side exit, and they descended the stairs to the alley. The livery was two blocks down, on the same side of the street. Train led the roan, and Crane walked at his side as they maneuvered through a back alley before crossing a secondary street that led to the livery. The door was open, and there was a lamp on inside. Train peered through the crack in the door. He saw the ostler, working with a harness near one of the stalls. Otherwise, the stable seemed empty. Train nodded to Crane, and the two of them entered.

The ostler looked up. He was about fifty, wore worn clothes, a battered Stetson, and dirty boots. "What can I do for you gents?" he asked as he eyed them closely.

"I need a trail horse. Have you got any for sale?" Train inquired.

"Sure. I can part with that gray over there in that second stall for forty. A saddle will be twenty extra. I'll throw in the harness."

Train glanced at the horse and nodded. He reached into his pocket and fished out the cash, which he handed over to the stableman.

An almost greedy expression crossed the man's face as he folded the bills and placed them into his shirt pocket. "I'll saddle him up for you," he said, pulling a saddle from a frame.

"I'll do it. We're in a hurry. Just get me the bill of sale," Train directed.

"Whatever you say," the ostler said as he made his way to his office.

Train backed the gray out of the stall and tossed on a blanket and the saddle. He tightened the cinch and then selected a harness from a peg. The gray was ready to travel when Train heard the cocking of a rifle. He turned to see the ostler standing behind him, pointing a Winchester at him.

"Don't even think about movin', Mr. Train. I won't hesitate to use this."

Train slowly raised his hands. "You know me then?"

"Recognized you right off. You're worth ten thousand dollars—biggest reward I ever heard of anywhere around these parts, and I aim to collect it, dead or alive."

"I don't suppose it would do any good to tell you that I'm innocent?"

The ostler grinned. "None at all."

Train nodded, and Crane edged away nervously.

"The sheriff's out of town, so I'll be holdin' you until he gets back." Careful to keep his eyes on Train, the ostler back stepped until he reached a shelf. Transferring the rifle to his left hand, he felt along the shelf with his right. He picked up a key, which he tucked inside his shirt pocket, and then hefted some manacles, which he tossed on the ground at Train's feet. "Put those around one of your wrists."

Train hesitated, but the sight of the Winchester made him obey. He knelt down, picked up the manacles, and fastened one ring onto his left wrist.

"Now, back up to that stall and sit down on the ground."

Train did as he was told.

The ostler stepped closer, transferring the Winchester back to his right hand, all the while keeping the barrel at an angle about level with Train's chest. "Put your arms around that corner post."

Train watched the man closely, measuring distances and assessing the way he moved. He placed his arms around the post, knowing that once the manacles were locked into place, he would have virtually no chance of leaving the town of Clayton.

The ostler knelt down and, with his left hand, removed Train's Colt from his holster and tossed it aside. He then checked to see that the ring was firmly in place around Train's left wrist. Satisfied that it was, he secured the other ring around Train's right wrist. In order to do this, he had to take his eyes off Train. It was the moment Train anticipated. He had just enough operating room to clutch the rifle barrel and pull it forward, jerking the ostler off balance and yanking his head against the corner post. There was a loud thud as the ostler's battered Stetson fell off his head and he suddenly toppled over.

Train reached for the key in the ostler's shirt pocket, but from his position, he could not quite grip it. He jerked again on the ostler's arm, pulling him closer. He then ripped the pocket from the shirt, and the key fell to the ground next to him. He quickly shed himself of the manacles and climbed to his feet. In turn, he placed the restraints around the ostler's wrists and secured him to the post. He then tossed the key into a haystack and retrieved his Colt. He placed the Winchester behind a barrel.

Crane was huddled in a corner near the door.

"Mount up," Train ordered. "I've had enough of this town's hospitality."

Ten miles outside of Clayton, Train called a halt and they made camp. He selected a spot where they were surrounded by boulders on three sides and picketed the horses. Following a meager supper of jerked beef, they lay down for a few hours of sleep.

Although he was exhausted, Train rested uneasily; not so much because he feared that Webb Crane would attempt to slip away during the night, but because he knew that they were in Apache territory. Even after he had left the scene of the attack on Ed Shamrock, he had seen the signs as he had ridden on to Clayton—tracks of unshod ponies. Now, they would be journeying even deeper into the land of the Apache, for Train had decided to take Crane to Warrensburg in the hope of making contact with Marshal Frank Weldon. He left both horses saddled in the event that they would need to move quickly, and he slept with his Colt in his hand.

Dawn came quickly and Train roused Crane, who stirred irritably. "What's the rush, Matt? I doubt that any-one from Clayton is after us. They sure couldn't track us in the dark."

"We've got close to twenty miles to Warrensburg, and I want to get moving."

"What about some breakfast?"

"No fire."

Crane shrugged. "No coffee." He raised himself on his elbow and ran his fingers through his tousled hair. "And to think that I could be back in that hotel now, having ham and eggs."

"Mount up," Train directed.

"What's the big rush? I'm not even awake yet."

"I've got an itch on the back of my neck."

Crane shot a questioning glance at him.

"Apaches."

Crane's eyes widened as he sat bolt upright and looked around nervously. "You've seen them?"

"On my way to Clayton, I came across some of their handiwork. Since then, I've seen their tracks."

"Well, what are we waiting for? I don't relish being caught out here in the open," he said as he climbed to his feet.

Within minutes, they were in their saddles and on the trail.

For the next hour they paused frequently as Train scanned the terrain ahead as well as their back trail. He avoided any spot that might have invited a possible ambush, measuring distances and considering avenues of escape before committing them to any advance. Despite his precautions, however, he realized that they were still vulnerable to attack from any number of places and in any number of ways. Nevertheless, he was desperate to keep Crane alive—at least until the man could tell the facts in the shootings of Sheriff Marbury and his deputy. After that, as far as he was concerned, Crane was on his own.

They crossed an open stretch of ground that afforded good visibility for a considerable distance in every direction but also offered no protection should they encounter an attack. Under normal circumstances, Train would have preferred just such terrain, for Bullwhip was a fleet runner that could outdistance any horse Train had ever seen. Nevertheless, the horse had traveled hard and far over the last week or so and was now performing on grit alone. He needed a few bags of oats and a good rest, something that Train could not yet give him. His strides were a bit shorter, and his head hung lower, yet he continued to respond to Train's commands with all he had. Once in Warrensburg, Train had it in mind to turn over Crane to Marshal Weldon and, if necessary, to surrender himself until Weldon could sift through all the facts of the case. Then, and only then, could Bullwhip rest before returning again to Questor. Train, himself, also needed to string together at least eight hours of sleep before climbing into the saddle again, for he realized that he, too, was starting to feel his sharp edge slipping due to his prolonged fatigue.

In time, the open landscape changed, giving way to rolling hills, rock-studded slopes, thick blankets of sage, and occasional clusters of ocotillo. Here, they advanced cautiously. Train was ever alert; Crane was sweating heavily, his discomfort apparent as he fidgeted in his saddle and mopped his pencil-thin mustache with his handkerchief.

It was at a point near the base of a rocky overhang where Bullwhip's ears pricked up and the horse shied nervously. Train patted the animal's neck soothingly and then pulled his Winchester from its scabbard. With one hand, he cocked the rifle and then swung it across his saddle horn, where he rested it atop his reins.

When Crane witnessed the action, he urged his horse up beside Train's. "What is it?"

Train raised his hand as a sign for Crane to remain quiet. For a long moment, he scanned the landscape and listened for any untoward sound. He heard nothing, yet he felt uneasy. "Let's backtrack a bit and go around this ridge."

Crane nodded. As he tugged at his reins, a whirring sound broke the silence, and an arrow struck his horse's flank. The frightened animal reared, spilling Crane before bolting off. It did not get far, however, for it stumbled as its forelegs buckled and it fell into a ravine.

Train raised his rifle and fired. An Apache warrior cried out as he tumbled over a patch of sage and rolled down a slope just off to their right. Train spun Bullwhip and moved toward Crane, who was sitting on the ground, too dazed to move.

"Get on your feet!" Train called out, extending his arm to Crane.

Crane regained his composure, jumped up, and clutched Train's arm. In one swift motion, Train swung him up behind him and urged Bullwhip ahead.

Another arrow shot past them, barely missing its mark as Train felt the rush of air near his neck. With his left hand holding the reins, he raised the Winchester with his right and pointed it in the general direction from which he estimated the arrow had come. He fired, and then kicked Bullwhip, pressing him to move more quickly. The horse seemed to sense the urgency of the situation and responded accordingly as he darted past the ridge with little regard for anything save Train's command. For the next few minutes, they rode as hard and fast as the terrain would allow, dodging rocks and cactus until they came upon a long, winding dry wash. Here, Train turned Bullwhip sharply, steering him down one of the steep sides. The horse responded magnificently, negotiating the near impossible grade despite the fact that he was near exhaustion and carrying twice his usual weight. They hit the bottom of the wash, turned sharply, and continued for some thirty yards. Here, Train reined in Bullwhip and instructed Crane to dismount. Train quickly followed suit, grabbed his canteen from the saddle horn, and slapped Bullwhip on the flank. The horse continued on for some ten yards, where the wash seemed to flatten out against a rocky outcropping. It was at this point that the horse stopped, whinnied nervously, and prodded at the sand.

Train took cover between a pair of boulders, and Crane moved in beside him. It did not take long before they heard the pounding of horses' hooves as a pair of mounted Apaches emerged from a turn some forty yards down the wash. The first one was mounted on a buckskin. He carried a rifle loosely in his hand. He pointed it in the direction of Train's position as if the barrel were an extension of his hand, and he fired. The bullet clipped the boulder in front of Train, sending chips into the air, showering him and Crane.

Train leveled his Winchester, took careful aim, and squeezed off a round. It struck the Apache in the shoulder, and the rifle flew from his hand. The warrior dropped his reins, clutched at his chest, and slumped over his horse.

The second Apache rode a pinto pony. He hurled a lance at Train in a high sweeping arc.

Train slouched down and watched as it glanced just over his head and shattered against the boulder behind him. Train stood up, levered another cartridge into his Winchester, and raised the barrel. He saw, however, that the two warriors were in retreat, the one helping his wounded companion back down the wash.

Crane wiped the sweat from his face with his coat sleeve as he looked down the wash, his eyes wide with terror. "How many more do you think there are?"

Train shook his head. "I don't know, but if they want to try to rush us in this wash again, let 'em."

Crane glanced behind him. "Do you think they could circle around behind us?"

Train eyed the outcropping at their backs. "They could try, but we're pretty well entrenched where we are. No . . . their best approach is straight down this wash—the same way they just came. We should be able to hold our position here for some time."

"Yeah, but we're trapped."

"We've got water, and there's some food left in my saddlebags. We can stay here for quite a while."

"And then what?"

Train regarded Crane narrowly. "We'll take one step at a time. For now, at least, we're alive."

Crane passed his hand across his lips. "Maybe we can sneak out of here after it gets dark."

"Maybe, but I wouldn't count on it."

Crane shook his head as he wedged himself deeper into the niche between the boulders, sinking down slowly until he was sitting on the sand.

Train rested his Winchester atop the boulder and wiped the sweat off his hands. He studied the layout of the wash, assessing how the Apaches might make their next assault. He concluded that there were few if any places of cover. There were no rocks or plants large enough to lend cover or concealment to a man. In fact, their position was the only one within forty yards that offered any solid cover at all. In that regard, they were fortunate. When night fell, however, he knew that the situation would change. Shadows would fill the wash, inking in each side for a distance of several feet, enabling a man to slither along the ground without being seen. Train took time to memorize the geography of the wash, the irregularities it possessed, the angle of each twist and turn, in the hope that he would be able to detect anything out of the ordinary once the light was gone. Darkness was still a long way off. Whether or not they would still be in the wash by then, it was a calculation he had to consider.

After an hour, no further attack came. In fact, Train had detected no sounds or signs of the Apaches. It was a game they played sometimes, to hit and run and leave their victims with a sense of fear and doubt as to what to expect next. In this way, they could exercise a kind of control over their enemies without even being present. The problem was that one never knew for certain if the Apaches were still in the area, lying in wait. A wrong calculation could prove fatal.

Train was still on his feet, the Winchester resting on the boulder before him. He glanced over at Crane, who was still wedged in his spot, his eyes closed, a strained expression on his face. Train regretted in a way that he had ever gotten Webb Crane into this position. It was only a short time ago that his hopes of clearing himself had been renewed; now, however, trapped as they were in this dry wash in the middle of nowhere, the chance of either of them emerging alive was slim. He had his own troubles. It was true that they were due in part to Crane's weakness, but Crane, himself, was not the cause of his dilemma. When it came down to it, it was his own actions that had put them here and maybe even buried them. If he was responsible for Crane's death—even indirectly—would he be any better a man than Crane?

Train's eyes followed the ground features, drifting toward the mountains in the distance, and then gazing upward into the cloudless sky. A lone hawk soared high overhead, appearing to hang in the air forever without flapping its wings. Train wondered if the Apaches might be watching it just as he was. He picked up his canteen and took a sip from it. The water felt good as it cleared the dryness from his throat. He nudged Crane, who opened his eyes and focused on Train. "Take a swallow," Train said.

Crane lifted the canteen to his lips and took a long pull. "What are they doing? Why don't they attack us?"

"I don't know. Maybe they're waiting for others to arrive. Maybe they got tired of the game and moved on."

"How do we know?"

"We don't."

"I've been wondering about why they shot my horse. I thought Apaches placed a high value on horses."

"They do, but you were on the move. The arrow that brought down your horse might have been meant for you. Then again, it's possible that they aren't after horses at all. They might be more in need of guns and ammunition."

Suddenly, Bullwhip started to whinny. Train turned and saw the horse pawing the ground in agitation. Train picked up his Winchester. He scanned the terrain in every direction but saw nothing. A minute later he heard the crack of a rifle. Crane sat bolt upright and looked around. There was silence again, and then a series of shots followed—not in the wash, yet not far off. Train then heard the pounding of hooves, followed by the voices of white men. He and Crane exchanged glances and refocused on the wash. Another five minutes passed and then a rider on a big black horse appeared, moving slowly in their direction.

"Over here!" Crane shouted out as he jumped into the open and started to wave.

The rider hesitated, spotted Crane, and then advanced.

Train stepped into the open and stood beside Crane.

The man approached and reined in his horse some ten feet from them. He looked down and smiled. "Well, if it isn't Matt Train."

Train let out a deep sigh of relief. "Frank Weldon. You don't know how good it is to see you."

The man dismounted and shook Train's hand. He was big—about six-foot-four—and wore a black suit and a large gray Stetson. He was heavily mustached and wore a badge that was engraved with U.S. MARSHAL. "Just what are you doin' out here in the middle of nowhere?"

"Actually, Frank, I was coming to see you."

"Is that so? Well, that's quite a coincidence because I was on my way to Questor. I'm mighty sorry I wasn't able to come any sooner but we've had a passel of trouble with the Apaches. I've been up north, gettin' settlers moved into town. I didn't even get Ben Connover's wire until yesterday," he said by way of explanation.

"I figured it was something like that," Train returned.

"Well, what in the deuce is goin' on in your part of the country that's caused so much trouble?"

Train pushed back his Stetson. "Well, Frank, it's a long story. I don't rightly know where to begin."

It was then that another man rode into the wash. He was smaller in build than Weldon but was almost an exact copy of him in dress and appearance.

"My deputy, Bill Sacker."

Sacker touched the brim of his Stetson. "They're all gone, Marshal. Hightailed it out of here like their breeches were on fire."

"Well, it looks like your Indian friends have had enough now that the odds have changed," Weldon announced.

Train nodded. "How many were left?"

"Four . . . one wounded," Sacker said. "I also found one dead a little ways back. It seems that they were lickin' their wounds a bit . . . and maybe gettin' ready to hit you again."

"I was beginning to think that they had gone," Train said. "It's been a while since they first attacked us."

"That's their style all right."

"Small pockets of Apaches have been causin' trouble all over these parts. The Army's involved now. Must be three or four patrols in the area," Weldon explained.

"That's sweet music to my ears."

Weldon removed his Stetson and rubbed his coat sleeve across his forehead. "Bill and I haven't had breakfast. What do you say we make camp right here, and you can fill me in on what's goin' on."

"Sounds good. By the way, this is Webb Crane. I can tell you the story, and he can color in the details."

Weldon nodded to Crane as he assessed him closely.

Thirty minutes later the four men were finishing the last of a full pot of coffee. Train had related the events of the past few weeks, and Crane had backed up his version of the shootings of Marbury and Barlow.

From time to time, during Train's narrative, Weldon shook his head in disbelief. Finally, he said, "Judge Foster, Sheriff Marbury, and Ben Connover were good men. It's hard to believe that such pillars of the community could be removed so easily. And I'm mighty sorry to hear how your ma and pa have been driven out of their own home and forced to hide like outlaws. Why, I've known Mortimer Train for better than twenty years. He's one man who helped bring stability to this part of the country. He'd no sooner break the law than I would. The idea that he'd kill a judge—even an ornery cuss like

Judge Foster—is preposterous. How did the residents of Questor allow this matter to get so far out of hand?"

Train shook his head. "Fear mostly. The residents are no match for Ralston's gunmen. And then, Ralston fashioned a pretty fair frame, one that created enough doubt in some to put his plan over the top. He forced people like Crane here to back up his story, and that was enough to drive a wedge between what looked like law and order and the Trains. It put Ralston on the inside and us on the outside."

"I think there are plenty of people now—after the dust has settled—who realize that the Train family has been railroaded," Crane put in, "but with true law gone in Questor, what can the townspeople do about it?"

"That's why Pa wanted Ben Connover to send for you. We would have gladly surrendered ourselves to you, but anything else would have been suicide."

Weldon nodded. He took a sip of coffee and then placed his cup on a rock. "Your pa did right. No man could fault him for the way he handled things."

"He usually gets it straight."

"Now, the first thing to do is to get Mr. Crane back to Warrensburg. Bill, you take him to town and put him under lock and key."

"Will do," Sacker said.

"Rest assured, Mr. Crane, that no man will lay a hand on you while you're in protective custody in my jail. I want you to tell your story to Judge Talbott."

"All right, Marshal," Crane replied.

"In the meantime, I have to check on some folks on a few of the outlying ranches. Once I'm assured of their safety, I'll drop by the county tax office and have a talk with Sam Corey. No man can be prevented from paying his taxes by force. Once he's informed of the circumstances, I've no doubt that a reasonable extension can be granted if necessary. I can recall a time or two when there were similar cases."

"That's a load off my mind," Train replied.

"Next, my deputy and I will ride into Questor and have a talk with this interim sheriff. What's his name?"

"Dub Parker."

"I'll inform him of the facts I've dug up and strongly suggest that I undertake any further investigation of this matter. I'll also have him begin to retrieve all the wanted posters carrying your name—and that includes telegraphing all the law throughout the territory. That'll take time, so it would be wise if you were to lay low for a while longer. In fact, you'd best return to Warrensburg with Bill. Judge Talbott will want to talk to you as well."

"If it's all the same to you, I'd like to pick up my folks first. I think I can get them into Warrensburg safe and sound. We can iron out everything there."

Weldon thought over Train's remarks. "Might as well. Your pa will likely have to give testimony too."

"What about Ralston?"

"Bill and I will pay a call on Clegg Ralston. He and

his boys have some explaining to do. And while we're at it, we'll find out about this matter in Denver he was involved in."

"He won't go down easy. He's got too much to lose."

"That'll be up to him."

Chapter Ten

Doc Harrigan pressed his face against the window of Marion's millinery. The interior was dark, and the CLOSED sign remained on the door. He was puzzled as to why Marion had not yet opened the shop. It was not like her to miss a day of work. Perhaps Della had developed an injury as an aftermath of the stage accident as he had suggested. Marion might be looking after her. If so, why had they failed to consult him? He decided to make the walk to Marion's house to see if he could be of any help.

As he limped his way down the boardwalk, he encountered Mrs. Ginger. Knowing that she frequented Marion's shop, he inquired if she had seen Marion or Della. Mrs. Ginger indicated that she had not and admitted that she was distressed over the fact that the shop was closed because she needed to purchase some ribbon. Harrigan touched the brim of his hat and moved along.

He found the door to Marion's house locked and the curtains drawn. He knocked loudly and called out for Marion and Della, but there was no response. Growing more agitated, he walked directly to the sheriff's office. He found Dub Parker on duty, sitting behind his desk having a cup of coffee.

"Well, afternoon, Doc. What can I do for you?"

"You didn't happen to see Marion Vale or her niece lately, did you?"

"No, can't say that I have. Why, is anything wrong?"

Harrigan frowned. "I'm beginning to think there may be. I haven't seen either of them for some time. Marion hasn't even opened her shop."

"Well, I wouldn't fret about it. Maybe she's decided to take the day off—you know, spend some time with her visitin' niece."

"They aren't at home. I just came from there."

"Maybe they took a trip somewhere."

"I don't think so."

"Well, there's not much I can do about it, Doc. You know how women folk are," Parker said, grinning.

"I know Marion Vale very well. She's organized and disciplined, and she's a serious businesswoman. She never does things on the spur of the moment."

Parker leaned back in his chair and took a sip from his cup.

"Well?"

Parker shrugged.

"Look here, Dub, I think that something has happened to Marion and her niece. The least that you can do is to get off your backside and start looking for them. Ask some questions. Do something!"

"All right, Doc . . . all right. I'll ask around. It can't do any harm, I suppose. Don't get all heated up over it."

Harrigan shook his head in disgust as he left Parker's office. The door rattled on its hinges as he slammed it behind him and stepped onto the boardwalk, nearly bumping into Charles Ames, who was walking toward his law office.

"Sorry, Ames."

"What's the problem, Doc?"

Harrigan's brow furrowed. "I was just telling that worthless Dub Parker in there that I'm a little concerned about Marion Vale and her niece, Della."

Ames' eyebrows raised at the mention of Della's name.

"Marion hasn't opened the shop, and they're nowhere to be found."

Ames paled.

"I can't imagine where—" Harrigan paused in mid-sentence as he watched Ames turn and walk away in haste. Harrigan shrugged and began to mutter to himself as he continued down the boardwalk.

Ames made his way directly to his office, where he locked the door behind him and moved behind his desk. He opened his lower drawer and took out his bottle. He poured some whiskey into a glass and swallowed it quickly, leaving him with a stunned feeling. Despite his commitment to Clegg Ralston, he knew that deep down he was in love with Della Dorn. He had never met anyone quite like her. He had tried to put her out of his mind; he had tried to forget the meeting he had had with Ralston and Kagen, but the thought of Della in the hands of someone like Lute Kagen sent chills up his spine. Now, Della was gone. There was no doubt that she was in the hands of Kagen. The gunfighter had indicated as much when he outlined his intentions in Ralston's office. The question was, was she still alive? Ames determined that he had to find out. He opened the middle drawer to his desk, shoved some papers aside, and picked up a derringer, which he held in his palm for some time, staring at it—half by design, half in desperation—before inserting it into his vest pocket.

Train felt a deep sense of relief since he had located Webb Crane and made contact with Marshal Frank Weldon. At least now he had legal authority working on his behalf. He was eager to return to his folks and tell them the good news, but he had been long in the saddle and was too weary to make the trip. He decided, instead, to stop by Slim Holly's place and take the chance on spending the night there. He could then pull out early in the morning and be with his folks by noon.

He was glad when he finally brought Slim's ranch

house into view. A light was on, though the curtains
over the windows were drawn, and he could see nothing
more than the dull glow of the oil lamp. He left Bullwhip at the spot near the barn where he usually secured
him and made his way silently to the house. He listened
for a long moment before he approached the door and
tapped lightly.

"Slim," he called.

There was no answer from within, and he tapped
louder. Again, there was no response. Suddenly, it dawned on him that he had not heard Slim's hound. He realized that he had allowed fatigue to override his
caution. There was something wrong. He started to
back away from the door. A creak from the far side of
the porch alerted him that he was not alone. As he
moved his hand toward his gun, something hard dug
into his side. He froze.

"Don't move," a man's voice ordered coldly.

Out of the corner of his eye, he saw a shadowy figure
standing just off to his left. A second later, Train heard
the cocking of a rifle. It took little imagination to realize that it was the muzzle of a gun lodged against him.
He reacted quickly, grabbing the rifle barrel and jerking
it away from him while, at the same time, pulling the
man toward him. He swung a roundhouse punch that
caught the man squarely in the face, knocking him
backward, dropping him to the porch. Train took a step
toward him. As he bent over the man, something hard

struck his skull. He dropped to his knees, lost sense of where he was, and fell over.

The first thing Train felt was the dull throbbing of his head. Then, he sensed a tingling in his hands. He tried to move them but could not. In time, he came to realize that his hands must be tied and his fingers were numb. When he attempted to raise his head, he could not. He had the impression that he was lying on something hard. He opened his eyes, saw double, and then closed them again. He heard voices but could not distinguish them. Again, he forced his eyelids open, attempted to focus, but could see nothing clearly. He blacked out again. Later—he did not know how much later—he opened his eyes once more and saw that he was lying on the floor, on his side. He could see boots moving about near him. One pair approached him, and a rough pair of hands took him by the lapels of his coat, and yanked him up off the floor so that he was in a sitting position with his back to the wall.

He saw Cord Renfro towering over him, his nose red and swollen and his upper lip cut. Renfro glared down at him with a baleful expression. Behind Renfro was a man Train did not recognize. Off to Train's right were Della and Marion, sitting next to each other on a settee, fear etched on their faces. Slim Holly was in a chair next to them, his face swollen and bruised, his eyelids heavy as he strained to look at Train. His hands were bound in front of him.

Train shook his head to clear it. He watched as the man he did not know stepped toward him.

"The name's Kagen," the man said.

Train regarded him closely. "Lute Kagen?"

Kagen smiled. "You've heard of me then?"

Train nodded. "I've heard that you're the kind of man who will do anything for a price."

Kagen's smile broadened. "That's an apt description. How are you feeling?"

Train hung his head.

"I was afraid I hit you too hard. You've been out a long time."

"I'm glad to hear that you're so concerned about my health."

"Oh, I'm not, but Clegg Ralston is. He's got quite a stake in you Trains."

"I'm sure he does. He's had an eye on the Train Ranch ever since he came to Questor."

"Well, that's between him and you. Me, I was hired to find you and your folks."

"It's too bad that you're only going to be able to fulfill half of your contract."

"That remains to be seen."

The sound of approaching hoofbeats caused Kagen and Renfro to look at each other. Renfro drew his gun and moved to one of the windows. He parted the curtains and peered outside. "It's Mr. Ralston," he announced.

Kagen stepped to the front door and opened it.

There was a brief conversation which Train could not

overhear, and then, a moment later, Ralston entered, with Burl Archer in tow. Ralston took in the scene and then grinned broadly when he saw Train. "Well, well . . . I never expected to see the big Matt Train trussed up like a Thanksgiving turkey."

Train attempted to clench his fists, but he could not feel them, for his bonds were cutting off his circulation.

Turning to Kagen, Ralston said, "Good work. Your hunch paid off."

"My hunches usually do."

"And what have you learned from these three?"

Kagen shook his head. "Nothing."

"Nothing? An old man and two women?"

"I don't think there's anything to learn. The women admitted passing a sealed envelope to the old man—after they watched me work him over—and he owned up to giving it to Train, but none of them claimed to have seen the contents."

A glance was exchanged between Train and Della.

"And you believe them?" Ralston asked dubiously.

"As a matter of fact, I do. When a man is being beaten to death, he's usually willing to talk. This one had nothing to say. Besides, he claims he can't read. As for the ladies . . . well, they did their share of pleading in order to save the old-timer, yet they still couldn't come across with any information."

"Hmm." Ralston pulled a cheroot from his coat pocket and crammed it into the side of his mouth. He fished out a match and lit it as he regarded Train closely. "Where is this envelope?"

Train grinned.

Renfro took a step forward and swung his boot at Train, who barely moved aside in time to avoid it. As it was, Renfro put a deep dent in the wall.

"Easy, Renfro," Ralston said. "He won't be able to talk with a broken jaw."

"Yeah, well, look what he did to me."

Ralston flinched at the sight of Renfro's face. "When the time comes, if he doesn't deliver, you can have him."

Train's grin widened. "I can guess why you want that envelope so badly, Ralston. If it fell into the wrong hands, you'd be on the run the rest of your life."

Ralston jerked the cigar out of his mouth and threw it on the floor. "Where is it?" he shouted.

Train chuckled.

Ralston reached under his coat and drew a small caliber pistol from a shoulder holster. He pointed it directly at Train's heart.

Train stared at him but did not speak.

Ralston's jaw tightened. Then, he turned and trained the gun on Slim Holly.

Train twisted uneasily.

"Don't tell him a thing, boy. I'm old and worthless. Nobody'll miss me," Slim said weakly.

It was Ralston's turn to grin. "You may be right, old man." He then took a step toward Della.

Marion gasped.

Ralston leveled the gun at Della's face and turned to see Train's reaction.

"Don't tell him anything, Matt. He's going to kill us anyway," Della stated firmly.

Ralston slid the gun barrel down Della's cheek.

Train's insides twisted.

"Well, Train, do I start to kill your friends one at a time?"

"She's right," Train returned. "You are going to kill us. Why should I tell you anything?"

"Let's look at this as a straight business deal. You've got something I want, something that can hurt me. And I've got something that you want. You give me what I want, and you and your friends go free."

"Suppose I tell you I don't have it?"

"Where is it?"

"With my father."

"Where is your father? Where's he holed up?"

"In the mountains, in an old hut he built years ago. He's been there for better than a week."

Ralston reasoned aloud. "You wouldn't have been able to show your face anywhere—not with the bounty I put on your head. With Connover dead, that means that no one else could've seen it—only you and your father and mother."

"That's about the size of it." Train felt some security in the knowledge that Marshal Weldon was already aware of Ralston's past in Denver and that Webb Crane was in the process of clearing the Train name. He knew that Ralston's end would come; it was only a matter of time, yet the only way that he could prolong the lives of Marion, Della, and Slim—as well as his own—was to allow Ralston to believe that he still had a chance of concealing his past and furthering his plot to gain control of the Train Ranch.

"Can you get it?"

"Yes."

"Don't do it, Matt," Della intervened.

"Stay out of it, Della," Train returned.

"That's right, Della, stay out of it," Ralston put in.

"How do we know that you'll let us go?"

"You don't, but you can't afford not to take the chance. But as far as I'm concerned, you're through around here. You and your folks can leave—clear out of the territory. You'll have your lives, and I'll have your land."

"And what of them?" Train asked, indicating Marion, Della, and Slim.

"When I have what I want, I'll have no use for them. They can leave. They'll pose no threat to me."

"We'll talk," Marion interjected.

Ralston considered Marion's remark. "I don't think so. I own the law around here. Besides, anything that you say will be your word against mine. I can have a dozen men swear to the fact that I was in a poker game ten miles from here at this very minute."

"It won't work," Marion countered. "I have friends

in Questor. There will be plenty of people who will believe me."

"You won't be here to even discuss the matter. I'll buy you out. You and your niece can go back East . . . wherever you want to go. I'll do the same for the old man. That's the deal. Take it, or die here and now." His words were cold and stabbing.

Marion and Della looked at each other and then focused on Train. Finally, he nodded. None of them entertained any real hopes that Ralston would keep his word, but they also knew that every hour they could stay alive would bring a new hope.

Ralston smirked as he evaluated his situation. He felt confident that he held the winning hand. "How long to reach your father?"

"Four . . . maybe five hours."

"It will be daylight soon. You'll leave then. Kagen and I will accompany you—just to keep you honest. Archer and Renfro will remain here with your friends—for insurance purposes."

Ames figured something important was afoot when he saw Burl Archer rush into Clegg Ralston's office. His suspicion was confirmed when the two of them emerged within minutes, climbed on their horses, and rode hard out of town. Ames decided to follow. He made his way through the alley that accessed the rear of his office and located his horse, which he kept in a small stable nearby. He quickly saddled the horse and trailed Ralston and

Archer, keeping them in sight, but riding well behind. Despite the hour, he had little trouble following them and, within ten minutes, concluded that they were on their way to Slim Holly's place. He slowed his pace so as not to run even the slightest risk of being detected, and his patience and reasoning were soon rewarded when he watched both men ride up to Holly's ranch house and dismount. He saw the front door open, casting a broad shaft of light across the front porch. The outline of a man appeared in the doorway. Because of the distance, Ames could not be certain, but he thought it was Lute Kagen. The men spoke for a brief time, and then all three of them entered the house. Ames folded his hands across his saddle horn and watched and waited.

At first light, Ralston ordered Marion and Della to make breakfast. Reluctantly, they made their way into the kitchen and set about brewing some coffee and frying some eggs.

"Cut him loose. He needs some strength, and he can't eat with his hands tied behind his back. Just keep a gun trained on him," Ralston directed.

Renfro pulled a knife from his boot and stepped over to Train. Renfro grabbed Train roughly, jerked him away from the wall, and cut the ropes around his wrists.

Train clenched his fists and worked his fingers, but he had no sensation left in his hands.

Renfro sat on a stool near him and took out his .45. He rested it on his lap as he glared at Train.

Ralston, Kagen, and Archer sat at the table, whispering among themselves while Marion and Della set the food before them. Marion handed a cup and a plate to Slim, who looked a little more alive than he did the previous evening, despite the swollen condition of his face.

Della carried a cup and a plate to Train. He tried to handle them but fumbled, spilling some of the coffee on the floor.

"He can't eat. His hands are numb," Della announced.

Ralston glanced at her over his shoulder. "All right, feed him."

Della held the cup to Train's lips. He took a sip and nodded his appreciation. She then guided some eggs into his mouth. The food and hot coffee felt good going down, and Train responded to them in kind; yet his head still throbbed, his hands were useless, and on top of that he was bone-tired.

"Your story about the sealed envelope was smart. Most likely, it kept you alive," Train said between bites.

"You were quick enough to pick up on it," she said.

Train's eyes warned her that Renfro was watching them closely.

Della turned her head to the side so that Renfro could not see her lips. "You can't do this," she whispered. "You can't lead them to your parents. He's lying to you."

"I know," Train whispered back. "I won't do anything to endanger my mother and father, but I have to get out in the open where I'll stand a better chance. The way things are now, tied up, in this room, I'm as good as dead."

"But what can you do, unarmed, against Ralston and Kagen?" she asked, holding the plate near his mouth.

"I don't know, but it's a long ride. I hope to get my chance. At least I'll have only two to contend with instead of four. If I succeed, you know I'll come back for you."

She nodded. "I know you will."

"In the meantime, you and your aunt must try to do something on your own. The way things stand now, we may not be able to help one another."

"I'll try."

He smiled at her.

"By the way, Kagen keeps a knife up his left sleeve."

"Thanks. I'll remember that."

"There's no need for any talk!" Renfro snapped. "Just feed him and get back into the kitchen."

Della frowned. She held the cup to Train's lips one more time and regarded him closely, as though she would never see him again. She dropped her left hand and placed it on Train's hand. She did not know if he could even feel her touch, but she held his hand for a long moment before she released it, stood up, and then returned to the kitchen.

Ralston pushed himself away from the table. "Get him on his feet, Renfro, and tie his hands again—this time in front. He has to be able to sit a horse."

"He can't feel his hands now," Della protested.

"That's unfortunate, but I'm not about to take any chances with the likes of Matt Train."

Renfro did as ordered, retying Train's hands tightly, but in front.

Ralston opened the door. Turning to Renfro and Archer, he said, "If we're not back by sunset, it means that Train crossed us. You'll know what to do." He nodded toward Marion, Della, and Slim.

Renfro and Archer exchanged a knowing look.

Ralston eyed Train. "Outside," he said, jerking his thumb toward the door.

Train stepped onto the porch. The sun's rays were starting to fill the sky, chasing the scudding clouds and erasing the raven-black residue of the night. It was the start of a new day, yet it might also prove to be the last day for him and his friends.

"Mount up!" Ralston ordered.

"I'll need another horse. Mine is spent."

"All right, take Renfro's."

Renfro rode a sturdy pinto. Train approached it, put his foot in the stirrup, clasped the horn with both hands, and swung into the saddle.

Ralston and Kagen mounted and pulled up on either side of him.

"Here's the deal, Train. You heard what I said inside. You cross me in any way and your friends will pay the price."

Train nodded. "I heard."

Kagen leaned over and pulled the Winchester from the scabbard on Renfro's horse. Smirking at Train, he said, "Just so you aren't tempted to do anything foolish."

Train regarded Kagen narrowly.

"Ride," Ralston commanded.

Ames had stayed hidden in some brush not far from Holly's ranch house. When he saw Train leave with Ralston and Kagen, he had a rough idea of what was going on. He also saw Renfro and Archer remain behind at the house, which told him that Della and her aunt were, most likely, being held within. He calculated his chances of being able to free them. There could be more of Ralston's men inside, but judging from the horses he saw and the activity he witnessed, his best guess was that he was dealing with only the pair. The women were still alive, he concluded; otherwise, there would be no reason for Renfro and Archer to remain. He also wondered about Slim Holly. He decided to wait it out until the odds changed in his favor. He was no hand with firearms, and to face both Renfro and Archer would be tantamount to committing suicide, but if he could face one of them . . . that would be another matter.

Chapter Eleven

Mort and Sarah Train sat opposite each other at their crude table in the stone hut. Both of them appeared weary. Sarah ran her hand over the cover of her copy of *David Copperfield*, a faraway look in her eyes.

"What is it, Sarah? You seem kind of low."

"I don't know, I guess I'm just worried about Matt. He's been gone a long time."

"Well, Clayton is a long ride. I wouldn't say he's overdue. Besides, he may be having trouble locating Webb Crane."

Sarah nodded. "That's another thing. Webb Crane may not be too quick about changing his story. Unless he can be forced to tell the truth, Matt's trip may be for nothing."

"If I can get Webb Crane alone for a few minutes, I can get him to tell the truth."

"Oh, Mortimer."

He gave her a sheepish look.

"I'm also worried about the Apaches. Matt will be riding deep into their territory."

"Don't worry about Matt. He can take care of himself."

"But he was tired, done in."

"He's young and he's got sand."

She smiled. "He takes after his father in that regard."

"He's also plenty smart, and he takes after his mother in that respect."

Sarah placed her hand upon Mort's and then asked, "Do you suppose your friend Frank Weldon has arrived in Questor yet?"

"I don't know, but we could sure use him about now."

Sarah nodded. "Well, I don't suppose there's any use in speculating."

"No, we just have to hold on a little longer—until we hear from Matt." He eyed her fondly. "You've been a rock through this entire ordeal, Sarah. I don't know any woman with more faith or more backbone than you."

"And I don't know any man I respect more than you. You've worked hard all your years, and you made a grand home for me. You've been a wonderful provider, but I don't mind telling you that living in this hut and being on the run with you for these last several weeks . . . well, they've been hard, but I never regretted a minute of it because I've been with you."

For a long moment, they stared at one another, and then they stood up and held each other. Finally, Sarah pushed back a strand of her hair that had fallen onto her forehead. "Well, I must be a sight."

"I think so."

She smiled as if she were a young girl again. "I think I'll go outside and wash up a bit, and then I'll fix us something to eat."

"I'll set the table. We still have some airtights left and some coffee. We'll be all right for a few days anyway."

Sarah nodded. She picked up a hand towel and a bar of soap and stepped outside.

Mort placed some cups and plates on the table. He located a can opener and picked a tin of beans from a shelf.

Sarah left the hut and walked past the horses. She paused for a moment near one of them and placed a hand on his muzzle. "Well, how are you feeling today? Is your leg better?"

The horse nuzzled her hand and then tossed his head gently.

"Good boy, Jasper," she said, smiling at him.

She walked down a path until she came to a pool of water formed from a steady trickle off an overhang. Here, she rolled up her shirt sleeves, knelt down, and began to cup water into her palms. The water in the pool was cool and refreshing, and she enjoyed splashing it over her face. Within minutes, she felt better and she toweled herself dry. As she began to fix her hair, she chanced to glance up. Her eyes grew wide, and her hand froze in midair.

As Mort worked on preparing a fire, he thought he

heard one of the horses whinny. Seconds after that, he heard Sarah scream. His heart began to beat fast as he reached for his Winchester and bolted outside. He followed in his wife's footsteps, running in the direction of the pool, when he heard Sarah scream again. It was a shriek of terror the likes of which he had never heard before from his wife's throat. It was followed by a long, drawn out snarl. He knew the sound at once—cougar. He had no sooner brought the pool in sight when he saw Sarah running toward him. She was overtaken in an instant, however, by a large tawny cat that sprung at her and took her down. Sarah was buried beneath the wild animal, which appeared to be nothing more than a blur as it raged at its prey with an eagerness to kill.

Mort raised the Winchester and took careful aim. The risk of hitting Sarah was great, but every second that he hesitated brought the cougar's massive jaws that much closer to taking her life. Knowing that it would have to be the best shot he ever made, Mort held the barrel dead level and squeezed the trigger. The shot was loud. It seemed to echo through the mountains like thunder. In fact, Mort thought it had shattered his eardrums, for he could hear nothing afterward. He lowered the rifle and released his breath, not realizing that he had held it. The cat lay beside Sarah and did not stir. Sarah was stretched helplessly on the ground, her arm and neck covered with blood. Finally, Mort heard her moan. He rushed to her side, dropping the rifle on the ground and gently turning her face toward him. Her eyes were half open, her lips were trembling. There were scratches on the side of her neck, and the shirt sleeve had been torn from her left arm. Her arm itself was drenched in blood.

"Sarah! Sarah!" Mort called out in desperation.

She did not respond. Only her eyelids twitched as her breath came in short, quick gasps.

With tender arms, Mort picked her up and carried her back to the hut. He placed her on one of the bunks and began to examine her wounds. The marks on her neck were merely superficial, but the cuts on her arm were deep, and blood was seeping from them. Her face was ashen, and her body felt cold to his touch. Mort stared at her in terror.

What Charles Ames had seen from his position in the brush, Snake Danford had seen. He was even more ensconced, stretched out atop a flat rock, surrounded by scrub. Ever since he had ridden into Questor, shot up by Matt Train, he had kept his eyes and ears open, lingering in saloons, conversing freely with Ralston's men. His shoulder remained sore, and he carried it in a sling, which became a badge of honor to some, since he had obtained it in a confrontation with Train. Of course, his version of his encounter with Train differed considerably from reality, and it served to fuel Ralston's cause among some of the townsmen. Danford took advantage of his small circle of admirers, who plied him with drinks and information.

Like Ames, Danford had witnessed Archer's sudden arrival at Ralston's office. When he saw the two of them leave town at so late an hour, he was shrewd enough to discern that something was materializing. He was aware that anything concerning Ralston translated into potential money, and money was his main interest. He was even more curious when he saw Charles Ames, the attorney, follow after Ralston. Danford could not resist knowing what was of such interest to so many. He determined to find out.

Danford had no knowledge of what was going on in the ranch house. He did not know why Archer and Renfro remained behind, but when he saw Matt Train with his hands tied and Ralston and Kagen riding alongside him, he drew his own conclusions. He watched them for some time through his binoculars until they reached the foothills in the distance. He then swung the lenses back toward Ames, who remained where he was, his eyes still glued to the ranch house.

Danford slid backward off the rock, moving awkwardly because of his shoulder. He backtracked to where he had left his horse. He could not use his rifle in the state his arm was in, but he could still handle a .45 with better than average skill—with either hand. He always packed a second handgun in his saddlebag. He removed it and tucked it under his belt. He mounted and rode off toward the mountains, in the same direction Train and the others had taken.

An hour later, Danford reined in his horse and pulled

out his binoculars again, observing the small party as they rode farther and farther into the mountains. Ralston seemed to have matters well in hand but one never knew. Thus far, Danford believed that he had done well in ingratiating himself to Ralston. Despite the fact that he had failed to take down Train, he felt that he had drawn the attention of the emerging town boss and earned some degree of respect for his effort. After all, ever since the Trains had been at large, none of Ralston's men had even caught sight of them. A man of Ralston's position could prove to be a powerful ally. Danford was shrewd enough to realize that his days of hunting bounty were numbered. Now that he was wounded he would be out of commission for that much longer. He may not even regain complete use of his arm again, which could create a major handicap in his line of work. That was another reason why he continued to follow. He wanted a second crack at Train for what he had done to him. The wound itself had been painful enough, but the loss of $10,000—the largest bounty he had ever pursued—had left him with a bitter taste.

The three men traveled in file, with Train in the lead, Kagen close behind, and Ralston further back. As Train rode, he assessed his situation. It was not good. From the onset, he had no intention of leading Ralston anywhere near his mother and father. He was simply content with leading him into the open, where he could expand his opportunities of escape. In so doing, he also reduced the odds facing Slim and the ladies by half. Yet he could forestall the inevitable only so long, for he was existing under a time limit. He had to find a way to escape and return to Slim's spread before sunset to attempt to free Ralston's hostages. In a way, Train felt responsible, for the lives of three people hung in the balance merely because they had tried to help him and his family.

Train glanced down at the ropes around his wrists. It seemed unlikely that he would be able to work his hands free, for Kagen checked his bonds every thirty minutes or so. Kagen was cautious and cunning—a dangerous man to oppose under any circumstances, Train concluded, let alone when he was tied and unarmed. As he led Ralston and Kagen through the winding trail into the mountains, he came to believe that his only chance lay in the use of the land itself as a tool for his escape. Herein, lay his only advantage, for Ralston was a townsman, and Kagen was not familiar with the territory. One possibility would be to lead his captors far enough into the mountains through a series of intricate twists and turns and then simply lose them in an isolated canyon. They would find their way back, in time, but by taking a different trail, it would be possible for him to return to Slim's spread ahead of them and formulate a plan to free Slim, Della, and Marion. Still, without a weapon, an assault on Renfro and Archer would be highly risky.

Another idea would be to overcome Ralston and use

him as a bargaining chip to free the hostages. That would be easier said than done.

There was one other point in his favor. With his hands now tied in front of him instead of behind his back, his shoulders and arms were under less strain; furthermore, some of the sensation was returning to his hands as he continued to work his fingers.

As they rode, Train contemplated the lay of the land, recalling every ravine and pass that lay ahead, any feature that might work to his benefit in freeing himself from Ralston. Finally, he concluded that there was one location that might afford him an opportunity—the wind caves. Actually, they were a good hour's ride farther than he wanted to take Ralston, for another hour's ride meant an additional hour on the return; still, the caves presented the only possible physical escape that he could imagine. He decided to lead Ralston and Kagen in that direction.

The men conversed sparingly as they traveled, for each was consumed with his own thoughts. Ralston was intent on retrieving the information that he suspected could cause his ruin; Kagen was determined to earn his blood money; Train wondered whether or not he and his friends would survive the day. Train found himself thinking about Della. She was steady despite the ordeal she faced. She was brave, having warned him about Kagen. He had never met anyone quite like her before. She was the kind of woman he wanted beside him. He thought it ironic that after he had drawn such a conclusion, he might never see her again. Thoughts of her kept running through his head as he rode on. There was something else that troubled him. From time to time, he glanced back over his shoulder, observing Ralston and Kagen as they rode behind him, studying the way they moved, measuring distances. On one occasion, he thought he spotted a whirl of dust far off in the distance. He considered that he could have been wrong. He could not imagine anyone dogging their trail into the mountains. Perhaps it was a lone Apache seeking refuge far from the soldiers. He concluded that he could ill afford to concern himself with whoever or whatever it was, for his problems were more immediate. He pushed it out of his mind and concentrated solely on dealing with Ralston and Kagen. As yet, he had no definite plan in mind, but he knew that he needed to formulate one before they reached the wind caves.

They climbed for some time until the terrain leveled off and they entered a deep canyon, the sides of which were steep and jagged. The walls were without relief save for occasional sprigs of brush that grew out of tiny fissures in the rock. The canyon floor was basically flat, although shattered boulders were strewn about as though they had fallen from a great height and landed with a tremendous force that caused their obliteration. Train urged the horse forward, picking his way around the rock fragments and growths of cactus. The others followed closely, watching Train intently with each twist and turn he took.

Train paused and looked upward. The caves were just

ahead. He had been here before many times. His father had first brought him here when he was a boy. They had always fascinated him. The result of erosion, they extended deep into the mountains, cutting through rock with ageless patience. The wind worked its way through the caves, sometimes whistling softly, sometimes howling like a wounded animal.

Train pushed on. When he reached a spot about ten feet from the base of one wall of the canyon, Kagen called for him to halt. Train reined in the horse and turned.

Kagen rode ahead and paused a foot away from a narrow crevice in the canyon wall, barely wide enough for a rider to snake through. "What's this?" he asked, suspicion in his voice.

"It's the opening to what's called the wind caves. It's a crevice that works its way through the mountain. It comes out about a quarter of a mile from where my pa is holed up."

Ralston brought up his horse alongside Train's and eyed the slight opening.

"I don't like it," Kagen said. "It's too close, and there's not much light in there."

"There's light enough," Train explained. "It isn't a true cave—just a narrow cleft that divides the mountain."

"Isn't there another way?" Ralston asked.

"There is, but it would take several more hours." Train knew Ralston was far too anxious to wait that long.

Ralston ran his hand across his lips. "How far does this crevice run?"

"About eighty feet. Then it expands into a series of caves before it narrows again and angles off to the west for another hundred feet. From there, it comes out into a canyon similar to this one. This is the shortest way in—unless we go up and over but we'd have to leave the horses and climb. It's the reason my pa picked this spot."

Ralston considered Train's remarks as he scanned the walls of the canyon. "Scaling these cliffs doesn't seem possible."

"It can be done but I'd never be able to do it with my hands tied."

"Well, don't get any ideas, Train, because your hands are going to stay tied," Kagen shot back.

Finally, Ralston nodded. "All right, we'll go through the crevice."

"As I said, I don't like it," Kagen protested.

"I'm not paying you to like it, Kagen. Just do as you're told."

"Look, we don't know where this leads. We only have his word for it. He could be lying, trying to trap us in there."

"Considering the fact that he's tied and we're not, and he's unarmed and we have all the guns, I don't see that he holds any advantage. Besides, he knows that if he crosses us, his friends are as good as dead."

"When I'm on a job, I do things my own way, Ralston.

I pick my spots and make my own decisions. I don't like being led into the dark—even by a man whose hands are tied."

"I told you that this job involved risks, and I'm paying you well to take them."

"Money is worthless if you're not around to enjoy it."

Ralston's jaw tightened. "All right, suppose I sweeten the pot?"

Kagen's eyes widened.

"We pass through this mountain and we travel another quarter of a mile. Then, I get what I want. There's another five thousand in it for you if you see it through."

Kagen considered Ralston closely. "Whatever it is the Trains have you must want very badly." He then eyed the mouth of the crevice once again. He raised Train's hands and checked the rope. "All right."

Ralston sneered in satisfaction.

"Go ahead, Train, but if you make one false move I'll drill you," Kagen said, removing the thong from the hammer of his .45.

Train spun the horse and led it into the crevice. The animal shied at first, but after Train patted its neck, it advanced as directed.

Kagen followed, keeping a safe distance behind. Ralston, in turn, trailed him.

The crevice afforded the men and horses little room for comfort. In fact, in several places, they were forced to lean forward in their saddles to negotiate the low ceiling. The sound of the horses' hooves echoed eerily, resonating throughout the passage like muffled drums. Train had not ridden far inside the crevice when he loosened the lasso from his saddle. Using his body to shield his hands from Kagen's watchful eyes, he held the lasso loosely in his hands.

As the passage angled slightly at various points, Train knew that he was out of Kagen's sight for as much as several seconds at a time. He was counting on this to create the edge that he needed. What he had told Ralston about the series of caverns ahead was true. It was in the caverns where he was determined to make his move.

Train quickened the pace of his horse in order to put a few more seconds between Kagen and himself— seconds he knew he would badly need to put his plan into action. As he maneuvered around the last twist in the crevice, he sighted the first cavern just ahead. The interior was dim, yet not without some light, for the fissure ran clear to the top of the mountain in some places. The cavern was large and irregular in shape. At its widest point, it extended for some forty or fifty feet, but its exact dimensions were difficult to discern because of the heavy shadows across the floor. Train dismounted immediately. He turned the horse around so that it faced the direction from which it had just come, and then he slapped its flank. The animal bolted forward, filling the passage with its girth, heading directly for the oncoming Kagen.

Train then worked quickly to uncoil the lasso—a difficult task in itself with his hands tied. He scanned the cavern walls for several seconds before he found a spot that suited his needs—an overhang about twenty feet off the cavern floor. He swung his loop toward it. It caught, and he made tight the lasso. It was then that he heard the sounds of startled panic as a certain collision had inevitably occurred. The excited neighing of the horses in the passage filled Train's ears and gave him what he hoped would be the time he needed to conceal himself among some rocks on the opposite side of the cavern.

Train heard Kagen swearing angrily, and he knew the bounty hunter must be struggling to bring both horses under control. In the meantime, Train began to work on the ropes that still bound his wrists together. He found a jagged edge of rock and started to rub the rope against it.

It took a full minute before Kagen emerged from the crevice. He was on foot, his gun was drawn, and there was a look of exasperation on his face as his eyes darted back and forth, searching the cavern. A moment later, Ralston followed him in, his gun in his hand as well, his face burning with rage.

"There!" Ralston shouted, pointing at the rope that hung from the shadowy overhang. "Get him! Get after him!"

Kagen slipped his gun back into its holster and stepped toward the dangling rope. Gripping it, he used the cavern wall as leverage against his feet and began to scale the slope.

Ralston stood near him, pointing his .45 upward as he peered intently at the overhang.

Train's bonds were far from being cut, yet he could wait no longer. He rose from his position and slipped noiselessly through the rocks.

Ralston was too preoccupied to notice Train's approach. Train was already upon him before Ralston turned and saw Train's clasped hands bearing down on him. The blow struck Ralston's neck, his body jerked spasmodically, and he fell to the ground like a sack of grain. Train then picked up Ralston's .45. Taking careful aim, he leveled the barrel at a point just inches above Kagen's head. He fired and the shot seemed to echo throughout the entire mountain. The bullet severed the rope, and Kagen fell backward, landing on the cavern floor with a thud that sent a cloud of dust high into the air. He lay there and did not move.

Train quickly moved toward him. He lifted the .45 from Kagen's holster and tossed it aside.

Kagen began to stir, slowly sat up, and rolled his head. He turned and saw Train standing over him, a gun in his hand. "Nice, Train . . . very nice. I'm not tricked by many men, but you played it clever."

"Get up, Kagen. Get on your feet."

"I . . . I don't know if I can. I fell pretty hard on my shoulder. It might be broken," he said, gritting his teeth as he tried to climb off the ground. He massaged his shoulder, running his hand slowly down his arm. When his hand reached the bottom of his coat sleeve, he inserted his fingers under his shirt cuff.

Train fired the .45 again.

Kagen cried out in pain, clutching his hand. At his feet lay the shattered blade of his knife.

Chapter Twelve

Cord Renfro and Burl Archer spent most of the morning playing cards. They paid little attention to Della, Marion, and Slim. Slim was still tied, but Renfro allowed him to stretch out on the settee. The beating Kagen had administered had taken the starch out of him, yet he had yielded nothing as far as the Train family was concerned. He seemed to be more coherent, and he managed to keep down a little breakfast, but he was hurt and sore and barely able to move. Della and Marion sat beside him and placed cold compresses on his face as he slipped in and out of consciousness.

Along about noon Archer seemed to grow short-tempered. He had been losing money steadily, and he had harsh words for Renfro. Renfro said little in return. He merely crammed a pile of loose bills into his shirt pocket and dealt still another hand. At last, Archer threw down his cards in disgust and pushed away from the table.

"I'll be back in a couple of hours—with more money!" he snapped.

"I'll be here," Renfro returned, grinning, "and bring a bottle. I'm gettin' thirsty."

Archer shot a disgusted sneer at him and stormed out of the room, slamming the door behind him.

Renfro burst out laughing. "That Archer . . . he never was any good at cards. He never could tell when he was being cheated."

Della and Marion looked at each other in disgust.

About ten minutes later, they heard a horse approaching. Renfro got up from his chair and pulled his gun. He moved to the window and parted the curtain. Then, a smile curled his lips and he holstered the weapon. He opened the door and in walked Charles Ames.

"Charles!" Della called out excitedly.

Ames' expression was serious as he glanced at Della but did not speak. He eyed Marion and Slim and then looked away from them.

"What are you doin' out here, Ames?" Renfro asked.

"Before he left town, Ralston asked me to come out this way and check on things."

"Is that right?"

Ames nodded.

"Well, as you can see, everything is under control."

"Charles! Surely, you're not a party to this?" Della uttered.

"Sorry, Della, but business, like politics, sometimes makes for strange bedfellows."

Della stared at him in disbelief.

Turning to Renfro, Ames said, "I passed Archer on the road coming out. He said that the two of you could use a break. Why don't you ride into town and get a few hours rest? I'll be glad to take over here."

"You?" Renfro grinned. "Your specialty is law books—not guns."

"I can't imagine I'll have too much trouble with a beaten up old man and two women."

Renfro ran his hand across his chin. "I reckon not, but . . . no, my orders are to stay here until sunset, and those orders came from Mr. Ralston himself."

Ames shrugged. "Suit yourself, but I've got some time to kill, and I don't mind staying. You can go into the bedroom and stretch out for a while if you're of a mind to. That way, you'll still be here if you're needed."

Renfro considered the idea as he looked at Della, Marion, and Slim. "I suppose that would be all right. Don't get too close to 'em and give a call if they try anything."

"Right."

Renfro went into the bedroom and closed the door.

Ames turned toward the others and held his finger up to his lips.

Della and Marion glanced at each other.

Ames then waited a full minute before he approached them, kneeling down on one knee. In a voice barely above a whisper, he said, "I've come to get you out of here."

"Charles, I—"

"Don't talk, Della. Renfro may overhear us. Is Slim able to ride?"

"I don't think so," Marion answered.

Ames frowned. "Then, we have no choice but to leave him here for the time being."

"We can't do that," Della whispered back. "We can't leave Slim behind."

"Della, I came to get you out of this, and I don't intend to leave without you."

"He's right, Miss Della," Slim mumbled. "You and your aunt go on and get out of here. Don't worry about me. I won't be any worse for wear by lyin' here in my own parlor."

"No, Slim—" Marion started to protest.

Slim held up his hand. "Miss Marion, you and Della have got some years ahead of you. I'm near the end of the line. Besides, I don't like the idea of a pack of coyotes comin' into my own house and runnin' me out."

Marion and Della eyed each other.

"Come on, we have to get out of here before Archer gets back," Ames said.

"Where will we go?" Marion asked.

"Well, we can't return to Questor. We can hide out in the mountains if we have to, or we can try going on to the next town. Wherever we are, we'll be safer than if we're here. Once we get to some honest law, we can do something about Slim."

Marion nodded to Della. She kissed Slim on the forehead and rose to her feet. Della stood beside her. "All right, Charles. I'm sure you're right."

Ames took Della by the hand and led her toward the door. Marion tiptoed right behind them. When they were halfway across the room, Ames paused and turned toward the bedroom. The door was still closed. He continued on. Slowly, he opened the front door so as not to make even the slightest sound. The hinges creaked, and Ames hesitated, glancing again over his shoulder. The bedroom was still silent. With any luck, he figured that Renfro was asleep. He nodded to Della and Marion, and then opened the door the rest of the way. Renfro was standing on the porch, facing him, a .45 in his hand.

Della gasped, and Marion pressed her hand to her mouth.

An angry sneer crossed Renfro's lips, and the scar across his forehead seemed to jump. "Get back inside," he said coldly.

Ames felt Della's hand grip his tightly as he backed up, moving slowly into the parlor.

"Something you didn't know, lawyer man, is that Mr. Ralston doesn't trust you anymore. He's asked the rest of us to keep an eye on you."

Ames returned Renfro's stare. "We can make a deal,

Renfro. I've got some money. I can make it worth your while."

Renfro grinned. "No deal. Besides, what would I tell Mr. Ralston?"

"I'm planning to leave town. You can do the same. There are plenty of towns. The West is a big place."

Renfro shook his head. "I don't plan on runnin' for the rest of my life—not from the likes of a man like Clegg Ralston."

"Renfro—"

"Shut up!"

Ames moved Della and Marion further behind him as he continued to step backward, putting a little more distance between Renfro and himself. "All right, Cord, whatever you say." He turned his back to Renfro and winked at Della and Marion. Reaching into his vest pocket, he pulled out his derringer. He took a deep breath, exhaled, and then spun quickly. A shot erupted, and Ames fell backward into Della's arms. Marion moved forward, and together, they eased him to the floor. A small circle of blood on Ames' vest grew larger, and his face turned pale. His lips quivered, and his eyes closed.

Renfro stepped forward and picked up the derringer from the floor. "Serves you right, lawyer man," he said, looking down at Ames.

"Charles . . . Charles!" Della cried out as she ran her hand across his forehead.

A moment later Ames opened his eyes. They seemed

to focus on Della. He attempted to speak, but he had difficulty. Finally, he said, *"'The hungry judges soon the sentence sign, And wretches hang that jurymen may dine.'"* He coughed and then forced a smile. "It was Alexander Pope who said it, Della." His smile faded, and his eyelids drooped.

Tears rolled down Della's face as she looked at Marion.

Snake Danford heard the sound of gunshots, deep within the mountain. He could only guess what they meant. A short time later, however, he watched with surprise as the three men came into view once again, with Matt Train now riding behind Ralston and Kagen. Ralston and Kagen were now the captives, bound securely, barely able to use even their hands in holding on to their reins. Both men were disheveled, their faces drawn and strained. Kagen's hand was wrapped in a bloody bandanna. By some quirk of fate, the situation had suddenly changed, and Danford found himself in an interesting position. He lowered his binoculars and laughed inwardly, shaking his head in disbelief as he thanked lady luck for giving him this opportunity. Not only was he primed to kill Matt Train but he was also in line to save Clegg Ralston from Train's gun. Extricating Ralston could prove a feather in his cap and permanently establish himself as an integral part of Ralston's organization. Danford actually licked his lips as he mused at the possibilities that had just been presented to him.

The men rode in the same direction that would take them back to the ranch house they had left at sunrise. Danford recalled the terrain and quickly calculated time and distance. He mounted and rode aggressively, and in ten minutes arrived at a position that would prove perfect for an ambush. He dismounted behind a large boulder and secured the reins of his horse to the branch of a stunted pine. He scaled the spine of a long shelf of rock until he reached a position overlooking the trail that Train and the others were likely to cross. From this vantage point, Danford was not more than twenty feet above the trail. He removed both of his Colts and set them near the ledge in front of him.

A little less than a mile from the cavern, Train, Ralston, and Kagen took a sharp turn in the trail, which brought them under a jagged overhang that resembled an eagle's wing. They passed under it in single file, with Kagen in the lead, followed by Ralston, and then Train. Train carried a Winchester across his saddle, balanced just behind the horn. He was alert to the trail before him and heavily concerned about returning to Slim's spread before sundown. His concentration was broken when some scree trickled off the overhang and landed a few feet in front of him. In an instant, he reined in his mount and swung his rifle off the saddle. For a long moment, he scanned what he could see of the ledge above while straining for any sound. There was nothing. He reasoned that it could have been a small shift of the earth.

Landslides were not uncommon in the mountains. It may have even been an animal moving somewhere above. He gambled that it was unlikely that it was anything else. Either way, he could ill afford to alter his direction, for time was his enemy now. Against his better judgement, he urged the horse on, though now his senses were heightened all the more.

As the three men rounded the trail that took them past the overhang, Train heard another noise. There was no mistaking the source of this one. It was the cocking of a gun. He froze in his saddle.

"Drop the Winchester, Train!" The voice was hard and threatening, and Train thought that he recognized it.

Ralston and Kagen reined in their mounts and turned in their saddles. Ralston grinned when he looked up at the top of the overhang.

"I said drop it or die right now," the voice came again.

Train slowly raised the Winchester, held it out to his side, and released it. He turned in the saddle and glanced upward.

Snake Danford climbed to his feet, a Colt held in his hand as he leveled the barrel at Train. He wore a satisfied expression on his face.

"Good work, Snake!" Ralston said.

"Thanks, Mr. Ralston. I thought there was a chance you might need an extra gun."

"Don't kill him yet. I still need him. He's got something I want."

"I'm not goin' to kill him, not yet anyway. I just want

to bleed him a little . . . the way he bled me. Then, when you're done with him, I'll be glad to take him off your hands."

"It's your turn to drop the gun, Snake," a voice came from behind Danford.

The bounty hunter's eyes widened in shock as he half turned around.

Mort Train stepped into view and pressed the muzzle of a Winchester against Danford's back.

Matt Train breathed a deep sigh of relief.

"Drop the Colt, Snake, or I'll shatter your backbone," Mort said coldly.

Danford tossed the Colt over the ledge and raised his hand.

Mort then knelt down and picked up Danford's backup gun. He tossed it to his son, who caught it and tucked it under his belt.

"You're a sight, Pa!"

Mort smiled. "We heard the shots coming from the wind caves, and we figured it could only be you this far back in the mountains. We thought we'd ride over this way and see if you needed any help."

"It looks like I did."

"Your mother is just behind me on the other side of this ridge. She's hurt bad, Matt—got herself mauled by a cougar."

Matt looked at his father in shock.

"She needs a doctor right away. I was taking her when we heard the shots."

Matt dismounted and climbed up the rock shelf until he was standing beside his father. "Keep an eye on 'em, Pa."

Mort jerked his hand over his shoulder. "You go and see her. The sight of you alone will make her feel better. Don't worry, I'll watch these hombres."

Matt quickly made his way over the ridge and descended at the far side. He spotted his father's horse tied in the brush, and a few feet away he saw his mother, sitting on a blanket, leaning against a rock. He rushed to her at once.

Her eyes were closed when he reached her, her head turned away. She barely seemed to be breathing as he knelt beside her and took her hand. He saw the wrapping on her arm, stained with blood.

"Mother," he whispered. "Are you all right?"

She stirred slightly and opened her eyes. The simple movement appeared to be an effort for her. Turning her head toward him, she smiled when she recognized him. "Son, thank God you're all right."

"Stop worrying about me. You're the one who's hurt."

"Mothers tend to do that, Matt." She raised her arm weakly and drew him to her.

He held her closely. "How bad is it?"

"It hurts. Your father did everything he could but he insists that I see a doctor. I tried to talk him out of it but he wouldn't take no for an answer. You know how he is when he thinks he's right."

Matt nodded.

"I was too weak to ride. He carried me in the saddle."

"He's right. We're going to get you to a doctor."

"Son, we can't risk it. Think of yourself . . . and your father."

"Sorry, Mother, but now it's time to think of you."

She smiled weakly and then closed her eyes again.

Matt returned to his father. They stood side by side, speaking quietly to each other as they faced Ralston, Kagen, and Danford.

"She looks weak, Pa. I'm worried."

"So am I."

"You know there's no fast way out of these mountains. We'll just have to move as best we can."

Mort nodded.

"Some things have happened that you need to know. Della, Marion, and Slim are being held by Ralston's men. They're at Slim's place. If Ralston and I don't return by sundown, Ralston's given orders to have them killed."

Mort grimaced.

"There is some good news. I found Webb Crane. I also met up with Frank Weldon on the trail. I filled him in on everything, and Crane backed me up. By now, Crane should be in protective custody in Warrensburg, and Weldon and his deputy should be arriving in Questor today."

Mort grinned broadly. "Well, that's great news! Well done, son."

"Yeah, I thought that things were turning for us until

last night. I was on my way back and decided to stop over at Slim's. That's when Ralston's men jumped me. And now I find Mother like this." He shook his head in despair.

Mort eyed him squarely. "Stand straight, Matt. We're not through yet, and your mother needs us now more than ever."

Matt suddenly felt inadequate. His father's words had hit home.

"Besides, we've got Ralston now . . . not the other way around," Mort added.

Matt nodded. "How do you want to play this?"

His father considered the question. "You were headed for Slim's when Danford threw down on you, right?"

"Right."

"Then, we'll all go to Slim's . . . together. We'll figure out a way to confront Ralston's men when we get there. Besides, I'm not sure your mother can make it all the way to town on horseback. We can borrow a buckboard from Slim."

"That makes sense. All right, if you keep these two covered, I'll get Danford on his horse."

"I've got 'em," Mort said, resting the barrel of his Winchester across his arm, angling it in the direction of Ralston and Kagen.

"Get to your mount, Danford."

The bounty hunter frowned and then turned and started walking across the ridge.

Matt walked after him until they came upon Danford's

horse. Train went through the saddlebags but found no additional weapons. He removed the rifle from Danford's scabbard and tossed it into the brush. "Mount up," Train ordered.

"Why don't you let me go, Train. You've got Ralston now. He's all you need. I'm just a small fish."

"I said mount up. I'm in a hurry."

"Train, I'll clear out of the territory and never come back. You have my word."

"You tried to kill me twice, Danford. You won't get another chance."

"Train, I—"

Train spun Danford around, wrapped his left hand around the bounty hunter's collar and his right around his belt. In one smooth motion, he lifted Danford off his feet and slung him atop his saddle.

Danford's jaw dropped, and he gaped at Train in disbelief.

"I won't tie you down like the others because you've got a bad wing, but if you do anything other than what I tell you to do between here and Slim Holly's place, you'll find another hole in your head."

The body of Charles Ames lay sprawled on the floor. Della and Marion covered him with a blanket. The sight of his lifeless form saddened Della, but it also angered her. She regarded Renfro now with a bitterness that she had never felt before for another human being. After some time, she nudged her aunt. "There's only one of them now. We have to try something while Renfro is alone. We'll never have a better chance," she whispered as she leaned over to check on Slim.

"Yes, but what?" Marion returned.

Della frowned.

"How's the old man?" Renfro asked.

"Not good," Marion answered.

"Kagen did a good job of working him over. He's very professional," Renfro said, grinning.

"He needs a doctor."

"Not just yet."

"When?"

"When Mr. Ralston says so."

"He may not be back for hours."

"Those are my orders."

"But it may be too late by then."

"With two lovely ladies like you tendin' to him . . . I think he'll make out all right."

Marion regarded Renfro narrowly. "You don't really have any intention of letting us go, do you?"

Renfro considered her remark. "Of course I do. You heard what Mr. Ralston said. Once he's got what he wants, there won't be any reason to hold you."

"Surely, you don't think that we're going to take this lying down. You can't imagine that people are going to take your word in this matter against ours?" Marion protested.

"Maybe . . . maybe not, but it's proof that you'll need before you can do anything about it."

Marion started to reply but she turned away when Slim started to moan.

"How about something to eat, Miss Della?" Renfro asked.

"Why don't you fix it yourself?"

"Now, that's not very hospitable. We can make this little visit comfortable, or we can make it unpleasant."

"I'm not fixing you anything to eat."

Renfro climbed to his feet. "I don't think you understand, Miss Della. When I tell you to do something, I expect you to do it. I'd sure hate to have to break up that pretty face of yours."

It was then that Slim whispered something that Della could not quite hear. She turned toward him and listened closely. His eyes were barely open but his lips were moving. "I think Renfro might like some sugar with his coffee." Della stared at him, wondering if he were out of his head. Suddenly, she felt Renfro's grip on her arm as he spun her around to face him. His lips were drawn tight, and his eyes burned into her.

"All right," she said. "I'll make something."

"That's more like it," he said, releasing her. "I like a woman who does as she's told. Now, I want some meat—cooked good—and some coffee. I want my stomach full when Archer gets back so I can win more of his money from him. It isn't good to play poker on an empty stomach."

Della brushed past him and made her way into the kitchen. She started a fresh pot of coffee and then rummaged through the cupboards. She found some beef and put it in a skillet. As she worked, she began to wonder exactly what it was that Slim had meant. She glanced at him as he lay on the settee but his eyes were closed. Marion returned her look, concern and fear written on her face as she remained helplessly by Slim.

Renfro picked up his cards and cleared a spot on the table before him. As Della walked over with the coffeepot, he sat up straight and eyed her suspiciously, his hand sliding toward his .45.

Della placed a cup before him and poured the coffee. She hesitated as the two of them exchanged a long stare, and then she retreated to the stove and replaced the pot. As she turned the beef in the skillet, she glanced at the shelf next to the stove. She reached for the container labeled SUGAR and removed the lid. Looking inside, she stared at the contents for a long moment.

"Is that meat ready yet?"

"In a minute."

Renfro took a swallow from his cup. "The coffee's good, but I like it stronger."

"Sorry, I haven't had that much experience in the kitchen."

"I should've had your aunt fix the vittles."

"Maybe you'd like some sugar with your coffee?"

"Nope. I don't take sugar."

"It might make up for the fact that the coffee is too weak," Della said as she approached the table.

Renfro shrugged as he pushed his cup toward her.

Della tilted the canister and then suddenly tossed the contents into Renfro's face.

Renfro shrieked in agony as a shower of red granules poured over his face. He leaped up from the table and rubbed his eyes with his hands, screaming as he lumbered blindly about the room. "Water! Water!" he called out as he banged into one of the walls and then fell to his knees, holding his face in his shaking hands.

Marion jumped to her feet, stunned at the scene.

Slim sat up and forced a smile on his swollen face. "There's only one thing I like better than sugar . . . and that's my red pepper."

Chapter Thirteen

It was an hour before dusk when Slim's ranch house came into sight. Archer's horse was tied in front, and Bullwhip was standing next to it. Matt prayed they were not too late as they halted under cover some two hundred yards from the house. They had agreed that Mort would stay behind, keeping Kagen and Danford covered, while Matt would ride in with Ralston and attempt to negotiate the release of Della, Marion, and Slim. Matt's sense of urgency was great, for his mother was now barely conscious, her eyes closed, her head hanging limply as Mort held her in front of him in the saddle.

Matt pulled the Winchester from his scabbard and trained it on Ralston, who rode just ahead of him, still securely bound. Matt had it in mind to use Ralston as a bargaining chip in freeing the hostages. He concluded long ago that any attempt on his part to overtake Renfro and Archer while they were holding guns on Della, Marion, and Slim would be too risky. On the other hand, with a Winchester pointed at his head, Ralston would be forced to do his own negotiating with his men, knowing full well that Matt had every intention of taking him with him should anything go wrong.

Matt wasted little time. He approached the house directly and boldly, with Ralston a few feet in front of him. When they were about fifty feet from the house, he halted Ralston and called out. "Renfro! Archer! It's Matt Train. I've got a Winchester pointed at Ralston's backbone. Step outside."

Matt waited, but there was no response.

"Do your own talking, Ralston," Matt directed as he cocked the Winchester.

Ralston tilted his head at the barrel. He then looked into Matt's eyes. He realized that Matt was not to be reckoned with. Finally, he turned toward the house. "Renfro . . . Archer . . . do as he says. He's telling it like it is. He's got the drop on me," he shouted, an edge of desperation in his voice.

There was another pause, and then the front door opened and Della stepped out onto the porch. When she saw Matt, she smiled brightly. "It's all right, Matt. We're fine. Renfro and Archer are both inside. They're tied up."

Matt looked on in disbelief. He wondered if it were a trick. Perhaps Della was being forced to make such a statement.

Sensing his doubt, Della stepped closer. "It's all right, Matt, truly. We're all safe and sound."

Matt grinned. He ordered Ralston to ride up to the hitching rail, where he secured their horses. He stepped onto the porch and wrapped his arm around Della. Together, they walked inside, where he saw Marion, who threw her arms around him. Slim was sitting at the table, looking a little worse for wear, but smiling nonetheless.

Renfro and Archer were sitting on the floor, their arms and legs bound as they were propped up against one wall. Renfro's eyes were bandaged.

"Just how did you manage this?" Matt asked, pushing back his Stetson.

Della quickly explained how she overcame Renfro by using the red pepper. "When Archer returned, we had Renfro's gun, and we were ready for him."

Matt shook his head in amazement. On the far side of the room, he saw a lifeless form stretched out under a blanket. He looked at Della.

"It's Charles Ames," she said, answering his stare. "He was one of Ralston's men but he tried to save us. Renfro killed him."

"I see."

"He was a good man, Matt."

They exchanged a long look and then Matt nodded.

"And you, Matt . . . it looks as though you were successful as well. How were you able to overcome Ralston and Kagen?" Della asked.

"I'll explain later. Right now, I have to get my mother to a doctor. She's in a bad way."

"What is it?" Marion asked, sincere concern lining her face.

"She was attacked by a cougar."

Marion's hands moved to her face in shock.

"Oh, no, Matt!" Della burst out.

Slim pushed himself to his feet and stumbled toward them. Marion put her arm around him and braced him up.

Matt stepped outside and pulled the Colt from his belt. He fired it into the air three times in rapid succession. At once, he saw Kagen and Danford emerge from their position in the brush, with his father and mother riding right behind them.

"Slim," Matt called over his shoulder, "we'll need the buckboard to get my mother into town."

"Take it, Matt," Slim said weakly. "I'd help you but I don't think I can."

Matt waved him off.

As his father and mother approached, Matt reached up and took his mother's limp form from his father's saddle. Her eyelids were heavy, her face drawn. She seemed lifeless in his arms.

"She won't make it into town, Matt," Mort said. "The ride on the buckboard will be too much for her. She'll bleed to death."

Matt looked up at him, stricken with fear.

"We'll have to bring the doctor here. It's her only chance," Mort said.

Matt nodded as he carried his mother into the house.

"Take her into one of the bedrooms, Matt," Slim directed.

Matt quickly carried her into the nearest room and placed her gently on the bed.

Marion and Della followed him in, hovering about her as she lay there.

"Find some towels and bandages, Della," Marion instructed. "We'll do what we can for her until the doctor gets here."

Della moved quickly, leaving the bedroom and making her way to one of Slim's closets.

A few minutes later, Mort entered. He looked down at his wife with heavy concern. Turning to Matt, he said, "I brought Kagen and Danford into the house. I tied Danford. They shouldn't give us any trouble, but Slim has 'em covered just in case."

Matt nodded. "I'll go for Doc Harrigan right away."

"Maybe we should both go."

"No, Pa. It's best that you stay by Mother's side. It may help her if she sees you—even for a moment."

Mort pressed his lips together hard. Then, he acknowledged Matt with a nod. "Be careful, son."

"Don't worry." Matt grinned. "There's no one that's going to stop me from bringing Doc Harrigan back— no one." He turned and left the room.

Bullwhip shuffled his hooves in excitement when Matt picked up his reins. Matt swung into the saddle and spun the horse. Sensing his master's urgency, the big roan leaped forward and was at full gallop in a matter of seconds.

Darkness had fallen by the time Train rode into Questor. The streets appeared empty but he remained cautious, using the back alleys to avoid any contact with residents. When he reached the rear of Doc Harrigan's office, he dismounted. The alleyway was dark save for a narrow beam of light from one of the lampposts on the next street. There was no one about, and Train advanced to Harrigan's back door. He tried it, found it locked, and then knocked. There was a long pause before the door opened. Harrigan stood there in front of him, surprise written on his face.

"Matt!"

"Don't talk, Doc, just listen," Train said in a voice that was barely above a whisper. "My mother's hurt bad. She was mauled by a cougar."

Harrigan's face turned sullen.

"She's at Slim Holly's place."

"I'll get my bag," Harrigan said, disappearing into his office.

Train stood beside the door and turned to face the alley. In a moment, Harrigan returned, wearing his coat and carrying his medical bag. As the two of them stepped into the alley, Train heard Bullwhip whinny. He pulled the Colt from his belt and pushed Harrigan behind him. He heard the sound of footsteps and jangling spurs. A shadow appeared against a wooden fence. Train raised his Colt.

A large figure emerged, filling the mouth of the alley.

Train cocked the Colt and aimed.

"Matt?"

Train strained to see through the darkness, but all he could decipher was the rough shape of a man silhouetted against the backdrop of the alley.

The figure came closer.

Train breathed a sigh of relief as he released the hammer and replaced the Colt under his belt. "Marshal."

Frank Weldon walked up to Train. "I thought I saw you ride into the alley. What are you doin' back here?"

"I've come for Doc Harrigan. My mother's been injured."

"I'm mighty sorry to hear that."

"She's at the spread of a friend of ours. Ralston's there too. So are some of his men. We've got them hogtied."

"In that case, I'll be ridin' with you. I've got some of Ralston's boys under lock and key already but there's plenty more room in the cells. Dub Parker's cooperating. He and my deputy are watchin' the jail right now."

Two hours later, Doc Harrigan limped out of Sarah's room. He looked weary as he wiped his hands with a towel. "Sarah's going to be all right."

Mort grinned broadly as he slapped Matt on the shoulder.

Della hugged Matt, and Marion and Slim smiled in relief.

Weldon stepped over to Mort and wrung his hand vigorously. "I'm happy for you, Mort."

"Thanks, Frank."

"Now, she's not out of the woods yet. She's lost a lot of blood and she's very weak. She's not to leave her bed for one week. When she's able to eat, she'll need broth and tea . . . nothing else at first. Marion, can you and Della stay with her tonight?"

"Of course, Doc."

"Good. I'll be out tomorrow to look in on her. I'll bring Mrs. Petry with me. She's done some nursing for me in the past."

"Thanks, Doc!" Mort said.

Harrigan smiled. "She's a good woman, Mort. Take care of her."

"I intend to."

"Now, Slim, I'll have a look at you."

"Oh, don't bother, Doc. The ladies have been lookin' after me just fine. I'm doin' all right."

"I'll be the judge of that. Come into the other bedroom and stretch out."

Slim started to object but Harrigan walked up to him and took his arm. Matt took his other arm, and together they assisted him into the bedroom. They got his shirt off, and Harrigan began to examine him, poking and prodding him until Slim winced with pain.

"Well, as near as I can tell, you've got a couple of

cracked ribs. There won't be any more ranch work for you for a spell. You won't even be riding a horse. I'll wrap you up a bit and give you some pills for the pain. As far as your facial bruises are concerned, it looks like the ladies did a pretty credible job. The bottom line is that you're going to be pretty stiff and sore for a while."

Slim nodded. "I don't reckon I needed anybody to tell me that."

"You're welcome," Harrigan said as he winked at Matt.

When Harrigan had finished, he and Matt returned to the parlor.

Harrigan left some additional instructions for Slim's care and then announced that he would return early the following morning.

"I'll be ridin' back with you, Doc," Weldon announced. "I'm goin' to get these boys into a nice, comfortable jail cell. Matt, I could use your help."

"Glad to, Marshal."

They took Ames' body away and got Ralston and his men on their horses.

Matt took Della's hand. "Look after my mother."

"I'll stay by her side."

"I'll be back soon."

She smiled at him. "I know you will."

Some of Clegg Ralston's gunmen had fled the territory and remained at large. Most of them, however, had been arrested. They stood trial and were found guilty of various charges. All received prison terms. Cord Renfro and Burl Archer were found guilty of murder and were sentenced to hang. Lute Kagen was found guilty of kidnapping and assault and battery. Snake Danford received no prison time. Because there had been a bounty on Matt Train's head, all charges against him were dropped. Nevertheless, he left town immediately following his trial, having been threatened by a number of community members. Clegg Ralston, himself, was found guilty of murder. He, too, was sentenced to hang, but his execution was postponed pending an investigation into his implication in the murder of a man in Denver.

The long trials had proved to be an ordeal for the Train family as well as for Della, Marion, and Slim.

Della and Marion had visited Sarah daily while she was recovering at Slim's. They brought food and other necessities and kept her informed of the latest news in Questor. Sarah was responding nicely from her encounter with the cougar. She was regaining the use of her arm, although Doc Harrigan suggested that she would forever bear the scars from the animal's teeth. After four days, she was moved back to the Train ranch house.

Slim was also on the mend. His cracked ribs had proven uncomfortable, and he was unable to venture much beyond his front porch. In the meantime, Mort sent a few hands over to help out with the ranch chores.

The Train Ranch was operating at full strength again. The hands had returned from their cattle drive and were busy restoring the spread to working order. Some of the stock that had been driven off was recovered, and the balance had to be replaced.

Mort organized a rebuilding project, and that part of the ranch house that had been so badly damaged in the fire was nearly back to its original condition.

Della was preparing to return to St. Louis. She had been gone much longer than expected, what with her giving testimony at the trials and all the other events that had occurred, starting with the attack on her stage. Prior to her departure, however, she and her aunt were invited to a special dinner at the Train Ranch. She agreed to delay her journey until the following day.

Matt Train enjoyed one particular pleasure since his return to Questor. He took delight in standing on the boardwalk and watching the traffic move up and down the main street. It was a good feeling to be able to walk through town again without fear of being arrested or stalked by bounty hunters. Train had never been one to bear a grudge, but he admitted to himself that he would harbor hard feelings for a long time to come over the way some of the townsmen had looked upon his family. It would take a while before some people would be able to face up to him again. He decided that that would be something the town would have to live with. Either way, there would be no more running and hiding. That part of his life was thankfully over. Questor had changed since Ralston had come and gone. Perhaps it would never be quite the same again. Train knew that life for him would never be what it had been. Too much had happened.

He had had few opportunities to spend much time with Della over the last several weeks. The trials, his mother's illness, and the activity at the ranch had been a drain on him. Prior to that, the travel, the hiding, the encounters with Ralston and his men . . . all had taken their toll. He had been all but used up. If it had not been for his youth and his excellent physical condition, he would have caved in long ago. As it was, he was still played out and appeared toil-worn. His weight was down, and he found that he had to retreat to his bed more frequently and for longer hours. Now, he came to realize that she would be leaving. For some time, he had been thinking about Della. He knew that he was in love with her, but he had his doubts about several things. He wondered over and over again if a woman like her could leave a city like St. Louis for a small community like Questor. It did not seem likely to him that a woman of her interests and background could be happy in such an isolated area. Could she become the wife of a rancher? He had been wrestling with these thoughts for a long time.

On the appointed date of the dinner party, Sarah Train served guests in her home for the first time since her family had been forced to flee. She looked healthy to the point of being radiant, and she welcomed her guests with an enthusiasm that brought joy to everyone present. Mort had worked hard, and most of the damage that the ranch house had sustained was repaired. A thorough cleaning had made the house presentable and comfortable again, and new drapes and fresh paint brought life back to the Train estate. Della Dorn and her Aunt Marion were present, as well as Slim Holly and Marshal Frank Weldon. Pot roast, mashed potatoes and gravy, greens, and biscuits were the main fare, followed by apple pie and coffee. The conversation was friendly and relaxed, and for the first time in a long while there was laughter in the Train household again.

When the meal was over, Weldon leaned back from the table and loosened his belt a notch. "Sarah, that's the best meal I've had in years. I don't know how to thank you."

Sarah beamed. "On the contrary, Frank, it's only a small way of thanking you for everything you've done. You don't know what a wonderful feeling it is to regain your home and your freedom."

"I can vouch for that," Mort added. "Living like an outlaw was no easy ride."

"No, I imagine not, but you and Matt are still goin' to have to tread lightly for a spell. Some of those dodgers bearing your names are still circulating throughout the territory. You ought to be safe enough around Questor, where folks know the full story, but I wouldn't be too anxious to take to the road in the near future. You never can tell when some trigger-happy bounty hunter like Snake Danford will throw down on you without knowin' the facts."

"After what we've been through, I don't plan on wandering too far from the ranch for some time," Mort returned. "I'll be content to sit on the front porch and watch the grass grow."

Weldon grinned. "You've earned it."

"You won't even have to go into town, Mort, now that the trials are over," Sarah said.

"Speakin' of the trials, it was kind of interesting the way Ralston's men started to sing like meadowlarks when their bacon was on the fire. Did you notice how willin' they were to trade prison time by spillin' the beans on their boss?" Weldon asked.

"Yeah. Every man's got a little wolf blood flowing through his veins."

"Even Lute Kagen was spilling his guts," Matt added.

"I can't say that I'll be missin' him," Slim put in, touching the side of his face and then rubbing his ribs.

The others chuckled.

"You know, takin' a beating was bad enough, but when Kagen shot my hound . . . well, that was just too much for a man to bear."

"How is old Sticks?" Matt asked.

"He'll be chasin' rabbits and coons on three legs for a time, but he'll be all right."

Mort leaned forward and rested his arms on the table. "You know what bothers me more than anything about this whole matter . . . I thought we had plenty of friends in Questor, but I was mighty surprised to see how many of them disappointed me by throwing in their hands when the chips were down."

"Oh, Mortimer, you mustn't be too hard on our friends. Fear can do strange things to people—even good people," Sarah replied.

Weldon nodded. "She's right. I've seen it happen plenty of times. A lie can go a long way toward destroying a man or a family. It starts small, and then it gathers speed—like a boulder rolling down the side of a mountain. You add some pressure . . . some fear . . . and you've got the makin's of a full-blown landslide."

"At least, Webb Crane finally came forward and told the truth," Sarah said.

"Yeah, after hiding down a hole like a rabbit. The Train Ranch won't be doing any business with him 'til hell freezes over."

"Now, Mortimer. We have to let bygones be bygones."

Mort shrugged as he refilled his cup.

Weldon grinned.

"You may be right, Sarah, but even so, I'll not be buying many rounds of drinks in the near future. Speaking of which . . ." Mort disappeared from the table. When he returned, he was carrying a tray with a decanter and several crystal glasses. He filled and distributed the glasses. "I'd like to make a toast," he announced.

The others raised their glasses.

"To all of our true friends present who risked their lives to fight for the Train family."

They all drank.

"And I'd like to offer a toast as well," Weldon said. "To the Train Ranch, a true symbol of the West. May it stand forever, and may Mortimer, Sarah, and Matt Train live for many years to come to enjoy it and see it prosper."

"Here! Here!" the others chanted in unison.

In time, the conversation splintered, and the dinner guests drifted to different parts of the house. Sarah showed Marion her collection of old English teapots, and Mort led Frank Weldon and Slim Holly into the library, where they enjoyed cigars.

Matt and Della found themselves alone on the front porch.

"I'm afraid you didn't have much of a vacation, Della."

"I certainly didn't expect any of this," she replied, smiling.

"I understand you're leaving tomorrow on the afternoon stage for St. Louis."

"Yes."

Matt considered her closely. "I don't suppose that you could be happy in a small town like Questor?"

"On the contrary, I like it here very much. Aunt Marion has invited me to work with her in the millinery."

"But that's not the life for you?"

Della shook her head. "To be honest, no. All my training and experience have been in the newspaper business."

"We have a newspaper here. I'm sure something could be arranged if you were serious about staying."

Della appreciated Matt's suggestion but his words were not exactly what she wanted to hear. "I suppose it's something I could consider."

"I think you should. You're a brave, independent woman. This land needs strong people like you."

Della shrugged. "I don't know about being brave or strong, but there were times during this visit when I was plenty scared."

"I was impressed with you the first time I saw you—when you took on that Apache buck with nothing more than a canteen."

Della laughed. "I must've looked a sight."

Matt regarded her admiringly. "That, you did—quite a sight."

Della suddenly felt self-conscious. She averted his gaze for a moment and then asked, "And what of you, Matt? You have a wonderful family, a great heritage . . . you seem to lack for nothing."

Matt pushed his hands into his pockets and shifted his weight uneasily. He started to speak but he heard his father call to him. "Excuse me, Della."

Della nodded and she was left alone on the porch. She turned and took a few steps to the railing, where she rested her hand as she looked out over the corrals.

A moment later, Sarah came out onto the porch.

Della smiled at her. "Thank you for the invitation, Mrs. Train. It was a wonderful dinner."

"I'm so glad you liked it, Della," Sarah replied, strolling over to the railing and standing beside her.

"I'm relieved that this ordeal is over for you, and you're back in your home again."

"Yes, it was an experience I won't forget for years to come."

"Well, you and your husband and son are safe now, and you can lead a normal life again."

Sarah's eyes settled on Della's. She extended her hands to her, and Della took them. "Della, I think my son is in love with you."

Della's heart skipped a beat. "Oh, Mrs. Train, are you sure?"

"Yes, dear. A mother knows such things."

"But he hasn't said anything."

"Well, his father took six months to ask me. That's the way men are sometimes. A woman just has to be patient."

"But . . . I'm leaving tomorrow on the noon stage."

"I know . . . I know."

"But—"

Sarah squeezed Della's hands. "Have heart. If it's meant to be, it will happen."

Chapter Fourteen

Marion held her niece close to her and then kissed her cheek. Tears welled in her eyes as she looked at her fondly.

"Oh, Aunt Marion, don't get emotional. I'm planning on returning for Christmas."

"I know, but that seems like such a long time, and I just hate to see you leave. After what we've been through together, I can't help but feel that you've become a part of this town and the people who live here."

"I feel the same way."

"If you change your mind about staying in St. Louis, you know there's always a place for you here. I know you couldn't spend the rest of your life in the millinery business, but it is something you could do for a time until something better comes along."

"I appreciate that, and who knows? I may take you up on it sooner than you think."

Doc Harrigan stepped onto the boardwalk and hugged Della. "I came by to wish you a safe journey, Della."

"Thanks, Doc. That was nice of you."

"And to hug a pretty girl."

Della smiled.

"I'm sorry that your visit to our community wasn't more pleasant, but I do believe that Questor's best days lie ahead."

"You have a nice town here, with good people."

"I think so. Clegg Ralston wasn't really one of us."

"I know that."

The stage driver, Lud Barstow, approached them. He was about fifty, with long shaggy hair that dangled from under his Stetson. He had a rank-looking mustache, wore a buckskin coat, and carried a pair of Colts tucked under his belt. He was munching on a biscuit as he addressed Della. "Time to board, miss. You'll have the coach all to yourself."

Della nodded.

Marion handed her a bag. "I packed some sandwiches for you. The food at those way stations is dreadful, and the conditions are deplorable."

"Thanks, Aunt Marion."

"Now, you be sure to send me a telegram as soon as you get home. I'll want to know that you arrived safe and sound."

"I will."

Harrigan opened the door for Della and took her arm.

She paused for a moment before boarding and glanced up and down the street, hoping that Matt Train might be there to see her off. He was nowhere in sight. Disappointed, she stepped into the coach.

Harrigan secured the door and moved back onto the boardwalk where he stood beside Marion.

Barstow climbed into the driver's seat, threw some pebbles at the lead horses, and called out a loud, unintelligible command. The team started up, the coach lurched forward, and within seconds Della was being pulled down the main street of Questor. She stuck her head out of the window and waved to her aunt and Harrigan, who both waved back from the boardwalk.

Within minutes, Questor became smaller and smaller, until it was no longer visible. Della settled back into her seat and tried to find a comfortable niche in the cushions. Despite the jostling of the stage, she managed to take root. She smiled as she glanced at the bag of sandwiches her aunt had given her. She decided she would enjoy them later, when she got hungry.

Della's thoughts wandered as she stared listlessly out the window at the trail of dust created by the horses and turning wheels of the stage. She reflected over the events of the last several weeks. She thought of Clegg Ralston and Cord Renfro and how close she and her aunt had come to dying. She also thought of Charles Ames and how he had atoned for his involvement with

Ralston by giving his life in an effort to save hers. Mostly, she remembered Matt Train. She knew that she was in love with him. She concluded that she had been from that first time they had met. Such a thing had never happened to her before. She had never been the kind of woman who was easily drawn to a man, but there was something rare about Matt that she had never found before. He was thoughtful and kind, but in almost all of the time she had known him, he had been distant because of circumstances. Perhaps if they had met at another time, under normal conditions, he might have looked at her differently. It was true that his mother had claimed that he was in love with her, but perhaps she had been wrong. After all, was it possible for two people to meet as they had and fall in love with so much happening around them? No doubt, there were many things that Matt needed to forget, and in a sense, she was linked to those things. Maybe when she returned at Christmas, he would see her in a different light. Della pushed the idea out of her head as she leaned back and closed her eyes.

About ten minutes later, Della felt the stage slow and then come to a stop. The sound of voices brought her out of her reverie. Visions of Apaches crossed her mind, as well as another attack on the stage by armed robbers. Surely, she thought, another such incident could not occur.

Suddenly, the stage door opened and she saw Matt standing in front of her. Della gasped in shock. "Matt!"

"Della, I didn't want you to leave like this—not before we had a chance to talk."

"Talk . . . about what?" Della's heart was beating faster.

"About your staying in Questor instead of returning to St Louis."

"But I've already decided to return."

"I'd like you to stay. I've spoken to Joe Carson, the editor of our newspaper. He said he could always use an experienced newswoman. If that's what you want, you can do it right here. There's no reason for you to travel all the way to St. Louis. After that . . . in time . . . well, a man needs a good woman beside him—someone he can count on when the chips are down."

Della considered him closely for a long moment and then leaned toward him. "Matt, are you sure this is what you want?"

He smiled at her. "I'm sure, Della. I'll never find another girl like you. I want you for my wife."

She threw her arms around him and kissed him.

He held her closely for half a minute. Then, he heard Lud Barstow's rough voice.

"Well, what's it goin' to be, Matt? I haven't got all day. I've got a schedule to keep. Are you goin' to marry that gal or not?"

Della and Matt grinned at each other.

"Well, Miss Dorn, does Lud still have a passenger?"

"No, Mr. Train, he does not."

Matt wrapped his hands around her waist and lifted

her out of the coach. He set her down gently on the ground and slammed the door. "It's all yours, Lud. You'll be traveling a bit lighter now."

Barstow eyed the two of them and grinned from ear to ear.

"By the way, Lud," Della chimed. "There's a bag of sandwiches inside if you get hungry."

"Thank you, miss," he said, touching the brim of his Stetson. "A body does get a mite hungry on these long trips." He reached behind him, picked up Della's portmanteau, and handed it down to Matt. "You take care of each other now." He turned toward the team of horses and shouted out a command. They pulled away, and the stage lurched forward, leaving Matt and Della alone, engulfed in a cloud of swirling dust. They did not notice.